THE RUPA BOOK OF SUPER GENIUS SPACE QUIZ

THE RUPA BOOK OF SUPER GENIUS SPACE QUIZ

Dilip M. Salwi

RUPA

Dedicated to
a friend and well-wisher
Pradeep Dongree
for his helpful and friendly nature

Published by
Rupa Publications India Pvt. Ltd 2004
7/16, Ansari Road, Daryaganj
New Delhi 110002

Sales centres:
Allahabad Bengaluru Chennai
Hyderabad Jaipur Kathmandu
Kolkata Mumbai

ISBN: 978-81-291-0367-3

Fourth impression 2014

10 9 8 7 6 5 4

The moral right of the author has been asserted.

Hello! Spaceniks!

Spacenik? What is a 'Spacenik'? You may ask. Well, this is very much a quiz question in the book: A 'Spacenik' is a person very much enthusiastic to acquaint himself or herself with space activities. So, are you not a 'Spacenik'? The very reason you have picked up this book to read and know about space activities – one of the finest and thrilling endeavours of mankind – shows you are one. And this quiz book will certainly check on how much you know about space activities and how much you don't. I have added a scoring card at the end of the book to enable you to judge yourself and find out whether or not you are a genius in space science and technology.

I must add here that this 'Super Genius Space Quiz' is a revised and updated version of the questions related to space already mentioned in the previous successful book '1000 Astronomy & Space Quiz' published more than a decade ago. Of course, a variety of new questions have been added, especially about the Space Shuttle activities and Indian Space programme, which have in the last decade grown considerably. Today, when India is planning to send a space mission to the Moon, I am sure this quiz book would further stimulate interest in the subject among young boys and girls so that enthusiasm to achieve many more new ventures on this frontier does not flag at a future date in the country. After all, it is the enthusiastic, motivated and dedicated manpower who is responsible for a nation's success in any venture. With the hope that India, a land where rocketry was developed much before many others, would achieve many more feats in space in the years to come, I wish you happy space quizzing. If you are not already a spacenik, I am sure you would become one after going through this book.

August 15, 2003   Dilip M. Salwi

Acknowledgements

I am thankful to the following persons and organisations for supplying me the photographs published in this book: Asok K. Samanta, Manager, Archives, American Center, New Delhi; Malti Jai Kumar and Ravi Datta of British Information Services, New Delhi; Shiv Shankar of the CEDUST, New Delhi; Ravi Sharma of Federal Republic of Germany Embassy, New Delhi; and the Indian Space Research Organisation, Bangalore.

Last but not the least, I am thankful to my wife Smriti, daughter Neha and son Romel bearing with me while I was revising this book.

Dilip M. Salwi

CONTENTS

I

PIONEERS

First Astronauts

1. Who was the first woman to walk in space?
   (a) Svetlana Savitskaya
   (b) Valentina Tereshkova
   (c) Mary Cleave   (d) Rhea Seddon

2. Who was the first man to make an untethered space walk?
   (a) Bruce McCandless   (b) Robert Gibson
   (c) Valdimir Remek   (d) Valeri Ryumin

3. Other than an American or a Russian, who was the first to enter space?
   (a) Ulf Merbold   (b) Wubbo Ockels
   (c) Jean-Loup Chretien   (d) Valdmir Remek

4. Who was the first American woman to take a space walk?
   - (a) Mary Cleave
   - (b) Kathryn D. Sullivan
   - (c) Judith Resnik
   - (d) Christa McAuliffe

5. Who was the first Canadian astronaut to go into space?
   - (a) Marc Garneau
   - (b) Robert Thirsk
   - (c) Ken Money
   - (d) Steve MacLean

6. Who was the first private citizen selected by the NASA to fly aboard a space shuttle?
   - (a) Christa McAuliffe
   - (b) Norman E. Thagard
   - (c) George D. Nelson
   - (d) None as yet

7. Who was the first West European astronaut to go into space?
   - (a) Reinhard Furrer
   - (b) Patrick Baudry
   - (c) Jean-Loup Chretien
   - (d) Ernst Messerschmid

8. Who was the first living being to survive in a space trip?
   - (a) Able
   - (b) Baker
   - (c) Abrek
   - (d) Bion

9. Who was the first paid passenger in a space flight?
   (a) A Japanese   (b) A German
   (c) An Indian   (d) An Arab

10. Who visited the outer space as a tourist for the first time?
   (a) Rick Husband   (b) Mary Cleave
   (c) Dennis Tito   (d) Rakesh Sharma

Astronaut Portraits

11. Who is this elderly astronaut – the first American – to orbit the earth?

    (a) John Glenn
    (b) Walter M. Schirra
    (c) M. Scott Carpenter
    (d) Virgil I. Grissom

12. Who is this other elderly American astronaut who became famous in the early days of space flight?
    (a) Walter M. Schirra
    (b) Edward H. White
    (c) L. Gordon Cooper
    (d) Allen B. Shepard

13. Who is this astronaut with a 'first' to his credit?
    (a) Robert Crippen
    (b) Ulf Merbold
    (c) Valeri Ryumin
    (d) John Glenn

14. She is the first Indian – and Asian – woman to enter space. Who is she?
    (a) Kalpana Chawla
    (b) Sunita Williams
    (c) Kavita Verma
    (d) Jeniffer Mathew

15. Who is this young, charming and famous American woman astronaut?
    (a) Sally Ride
    (b) Judith Resnik
    (c) Anna Fisher
    (d) Rhea Seddon

16. Who is this astronaut known to almost everyone?
    (a) Neil Armstrong
    (b) Michael Collins
    (c) Charles Conrad
    (d) John W. Young

17. Who is this Russian cosmonaut, a household name in the early days of space flight?
    (a) Valery F. Bykovsky
    (b) Pavel R. Popovich
    (c) Andrian G. Nikolayev
    (d) Gherman Titov

18. Who is this space hero to have died during a space flight test?
    (a) Valdimir M. Komarov
    (b) Virgil I. Grissom
    (c) Roger Chaffee
    (d) Edward H. White

19. Who is this other famous man, though not alive today?
    (a) M. Scott Carpenter
    (b) Walter M. Schirra
    (c) Yuri Gagarin
    (d) Alexei Leanov

20. He co-piloted a space shuttle for the first time in space. Who is he?
    (a) Jean-Loup Chretien
    (b) John Young
    (c) Valdmir Remek
    (d) Frank Borman

21. He was the Commander of the 'Columbia' Space Shuttle that met with disaster. Who is he?
    (a) Bruce McCandless
    (b) Ulf Merbold
    (c) Rick Husband
    (d) Valeri Ryumin

22. Who is this famous space man?
    (a) Valdimir Lyakhov
    (b) Rakesh Sharma
    (c) Ravish Malhotra
    (d) Leonid Kizim

23. Who is this little known woman astronaut?

    (a) Christa McAuliffe
    (b) Mary Cleave
    (c) Anna Fisher
    (d) Svetlena Savitskaya

24. Who is this little-known astronaut with a first to his credit?

    (a) Marc Garneau
    (b) Ulf Merbold
    (c) Jean-Loup Chretien
    (d) Patrick Baudry

25. She was the Mission Specialist aboard the space shuttle that launched 'Chandra X-ray Observatory' into space. Who is she?

    (a) Christa McAuliffe
    (b) Svetlana Savitskaya
    (c) Rhea Seddon
    (d) Catherine Coleman

First Things

26. Which was the first artificial planet?
    (a) *Mariner-1*   (b) *Surveyor-1*
    (c) *Lunik-1*   (d) *Voyager-1*

27. Which was the first man-made object to orbit another planet?
    (a) *Mariner-4*   (b) *Mariner-10*
    (c) *Mariner-8*   (d) *Mariner-9*

28. Which was the first spacecraft specially designed to encounter a comet?
    (a) *Giotto*   (b) *ICE*
    (c) *ISEE-2*   (d) *Ulysses*

29. Which was the first communications satellite launched by the INTELSAT?
    (a) *Molniya*   (b) *Anik*
    (c) *Early Bird*   (d) *Telstar-I*

30. Which was the first spacecraft to travel to interstellar space?
    (a) *Pioneer-11*   (b) *Voyager-I*
    (c) *Pioneer-10*   (d) *Voyager-II*

31. Which was the first satellite to detect gamma rays from the deep space?
    (a) *Gamma-ray Observatory*
    (b) *Vela satellite*
    (c) *Einstein Observatory*
    (d) *Orbiting Solar Observatory-3*

32. Which was the first country to have its astronauts fly into space in both US and erstwhile USSR spacecraft?
    - (a) India
    - (b) Canada
    - (c) France
    - (d) Germany

33. Which was the world's first communication-cum-weather satellite?
    - (a) *L-Sat*
    - (b) *Palapa*
    - (c) *Midas-2*
    - (d) *INSAT-1A*

34. Which was the first interplanetary spacecraft launched outside the USA and Russia.?
    - (a) *Planet-A*
    - (b) *Giotto*
    - (c) *Vega*
    - (d) *Suisei*

35. Which was the first satellite to go into geosynchronous orbit, i.e., it stayed directly over one point on the earth?
    - (a) *GOES-2*
    - (b) *Gorizont-2*
    - (c) *OAO-2*
    - (d) *Syncom-2*

36. Which was the world's first space station?
    - (a) *Skylab-1*
    - (b) *Salyut-1*
    - (c) *Salyut-5*
    - (d) *Mir*

37. Which was the first spacecraft to photograph the hidden side of the Moon?
    - (a) *Lunik-3*
    - (b) *Ranger-8*
    - (c) *Surveyor-4*
    - (d) *Zond-3*

38. Which was the first satellite to be captured and repaired in space by the space shuttle crew?
    (a) *INSAT-1D*   (b) *Leasat-3*
    (c) *Telsat-1*   (d) *Solar Max*

39. Which space vehicle carried the world's first space traveller?
    (a) *Sputnik-1*   (b) *Explorer-1*
    (c) *Sputnik-2*   (d) *Vanguard-2*

40. Which was the first communications satellite ever launched?
    (a) *Gorizont-1*   (b) *Molniya-1*
    (c) *Aussat-1*   (d) *Telstar-1*

Pathfinders

41. Who gave the concept of the solar satellites that will beam energy to the earth through microwaves?
    (a) Dandridge Cole   (b) A. V. Cleaver
    (c) Richard L. Garwin   (d) Peter E. Glaser

42. Which satellite opened the field of X-ray astronomy?
    (a) *Uhuru*   (b) *Ariel- V*
    (c) *HEAO-2*   (d) *HEAO-I*

43. Who was incharge of the German V-2 (VfR) rocket programme during World War II?
    (a) Walter Dornberger   (b) Werner von Braun
    (c) Klaus Riedel   (d) Helmut Grottrup

44. Who started research on the solid propellant rocket in the erstwhile USSR in 1921 by founding a laboratory exclusively devoted to it?
    (a) K. E. Tsiolkovsky   (b) Yuri V. Kondratyuk
    (c) I. T. Kleimenov   (d) N. I. Tikhomirov

45. Who was the first to produce the design of a manned rocket?
    (a) K. E. Tsiolkovsky   (b) N. I. Kibalchich
    (c) Willy Ley   (d) F. A. Tsander

46. Who attached angled fins to the rear of rockets so that they became spin-stabilised and therefore could dispense with the guide stick?
    (a) William Congreve
    (b) Konstantin I. Konstantinov
    (c) William Hale   (d) K. A. Shilder

47. Who conceived of satellites in the truly modern sense?
    (a) Werner von Braun   (b) S. Fred Singer
    (c) K. E. Tsiolkovsky   (d) Sergei P. Korolev

48. Who proposed the idea of multi-stage rockets?
    (a) Hermann Oberth   (b) Robert H. Goddard
    (c) K. E. Tsiolkovsky   (d) F. A. Tsander

49. Which space shuttle was used for test flights?
    (a) Columbia   (b) Enterprise
    (c) Challenger   (d) Atlantis

50. Who gave the first engineering design of a rotating-wheel type of space station?
    (a) Hermann Noordung   (b) Von Pirquet
    (c) J. D. Bernal   (d) Arthur C. Clarke

51. Who proposed the need for developing standards for sterilisation of spacecraft sent to other planets so that they don't get contaminated with terrestrial microbes?
    (a) Bruce Murray   (b) John Glenn
    (c) Carl Sagan   (d) Sidney Coleman

52. Who proposed the idea of a European Space Agency for developing launchers and spacecraft under a cooperative effort in Europe?
    (a) Eduardo Amaldi   (b) Pierre Auger
    (c) Reimer Lust   (d) R. Reinhard

53. Who originally gave the idea of 'Mass driver', the electromagnetic launch mechanism for lifting mined material from the surface of the Moon?
   (a) Arthur C. Clarke   (b) Lee De Forest
   (c) Jay W. Forrester   (d) Johannes Winkler

54. Who was the first to conduct an experiment in space medicine?
   (a) J. B. S. Haldane   (b) J. D. Bernal
   (c) Constantin Generales (d) Werner von Braun

55. Who patented the system of space navigation that uses three pulsars as reference points?
   (a) Thomas Gold
   (b) Antony Hewish
   (c) Martin Ryle
   (d) J. S. Hey

56. Who gave the idea of the 'Space elevator' – a sort of lift to space, hung from a geo-stationary satellite?
   (a) K. E. Tsiolkovsky
   (b) Arthur C. Clarke
   (c) Krafte Ehricke
   (d) Yuri Artsutanov

Space Pioneer Portraits

57. Who is this American rocket engineer?
    (a) Krafte Ehricke
    (b) Frank J. Malina
    (c) Werner von Braun
    (d) Hugh L. Dryden

58. Who is this Russian rocket engineer?
    (a) Sergei P. Korolev
    (b) M. K. Tikhonravov
    (c) V. P. Glushko
    (d) S. A. Kosberg

59. Who is this father of modern rocketry?
    (a) K. E. Tsiolkovsky
    (b) F. A. Tsander
    (c) M. N. Tukhachevsky
    (d) Hermann Oberth

60. Who is this populariser of – and researcher in – space science and technology?
    (a) Peter F. Glaser
    (b) Johannes Winkler
    (c) Hermann Oberth
    (d) Arthur C. Clarke

61. Who is this space pioneer?
    (a) Hermann Ganswindt
    (b) Robert H. Goddard
    (c) Max Valier
    (d) H. F. Pierce

62. Who is this Indian space pioneer?
    (a) H. J. Bhabha
    (b) Vikram Sarabhai
    (c) Satish Dhawan
    (d) Brahm Prakash

63. Who is this Bharat Ratna Awardee Indian rocket technologist?
    (a) U. R. Rao
    (b) A. P. J. Kalam
    (c) K.Kasturirangan
    (d) Satish Dhawan

II

VEHICLES

Rockets

What are the names of these rockets and the countries that built them?

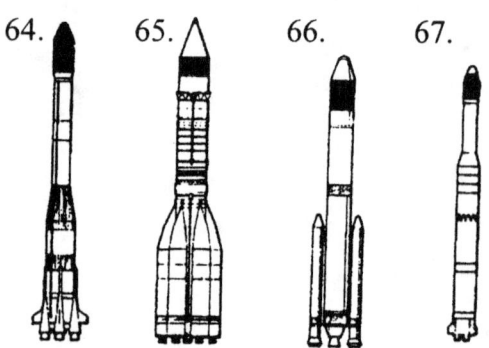

64.　　65.　　66.　　67.

68. Which is the first big rocket to be launched from the deck of a ship?
    (a) *Viking-4*　　　　(b) *V-2*
    (c) *RD-100*　　　　(d) *Viking-7*

69. Where was the rocket used for the first time as a weapon in a battle in recorded history?
    - (a) China
    - (b) India
    - (c) Italy
    - (d) UK

70. Which was the first rocket launched by a private company?
    - (a) *Conestoga-1*
    - (b) *Atlas-Agena*
    - (c) *Ariane-1*
    - (d) *Winkler-1*

71. Where was the first commercial venture to use rockets in different walks of life started?
    - (a) Germany
    - (b) UK
    - (c) USA
    - (d) Austria

72. Which rocket is lifted into an orbit of the earth by the space shuttle for launching satellites and spacecraft?
    - (a) *Titan*
    - (b) *Atlas*
    - (c) *Centaur*
    - (d) *Saturn*

73. Where was the rocket invented?
    - (a) India
    - (b) China
    - (c) Greece
    - (d) Russia

74. What is the term 'main stage' associated with?
    - (a) Multistage rocket
    - (b) Retro-rocket
    - (c) Booster rocket
    - (d) All

75. Where was the first modern rocket bomb V-2 built?
    (a) New Mexico   (b) Oldenburg
    (c) Peenemunde   (d) Dover

76. Where was the world's first hybrid (solid and liquid fuel) rocket launched?
    (a) Russia   (b) USA
    (c) Germany   (d) Austria

77. Which is the largest multi-stage rocket built so far?
    (a) *Titan-3*   (b) *Centaur*
    (c) *Saturn-5*   (d) *Atlas*

78. Where was the first institute established to conduct researches on rockets systematically?
    (a) USA   (b) Russia
    (c) Germany   (d) UK

79. What is a sounding rocket designed to study?
    (a) Space conditions
    (b) Terrestrial atmosphere
    (c) Night sky   (d) Magnetosphere

80. What are the small rockets on a spacecraft, space shuttle or space station that make small corrections to its flight path called?
    (a) Thrusters   (b) Retro-rockets
    (c) Verniers   (d) All

Satellites

81. Which type of satellite is placed in a geo-stationary orbit of the earth?
    (a) Spy satellite   (b) Weather satellite
    (c) Communications satellite
    (d) Early warning satellite

82. Almost all satellites obtain energy for their working from this. What is it?
    (a) Radioisotopes   (b) Thermoelectric cells
    (c) Laser fusion   (d) Solar cells

83. Which satellite system helps locate one's position on the surface of the earth within a few metres?
    (a) *NAVSTAR*   (b) *GLONASS*
    (c) *GPS*   (d) *All*

84. Which satellite was exclusively launched to produce an accurate map of the positions of 100, 000 stars?
    (a) *Hipparcos*   (b) *Giotto*
    (c) *Columbus*   (d) *LAGEOS*

85. Which type of radiation coming from space is absorbed by terrestrial atmosphere and therefore can be only studied using satellites?
    (a) Radio waves   (b) X-rays
    (c) Gamma rays   (d) Cosmic rays

86. How many communication satellites in geo-stationary orbit provide global coverage?
    (a) Twelve   (b) Six
    (c) Three   (d) Twenty-four

87. *Anik* is the name of a series of domestic communications satellites. Which country launched it?
    (a) India   (b) Thailand
    (c) Cmanada   (d) Japan

88. What is the purpose of a *Sarsat*?
    (a) Communications   (b) Weather studies
    (c) Infrared astronomy studies
    (d) Search and rescue ships and aircraft

89. Which satellite was used for measuring accurately the movement of the earth's crust?
    (a) *Starlett*   (b) *GLONASS*
    (c) *GOES*   (d) *LAGEOS*

90. What is the purpose of a series of European satellites, *Meteosat*?
    (a) Weather   (b) Meteor showers
    (c) Meteorites   (d) Oceans

91. Which of the following series of communications satellites is Indonesian?
    (a) *Orbita*
    (b) *Marecs*
    (c) *Palapa*
    (d) *Gorizont*

92. Which space observatory is likely to throw more light on extra solar planets?
    (a) *Space Infrared Telescope Facility*
    (b) *Hubble Space Telescope*
    (c) *Chandra X-ray Observatory*
    (d) *Mars Express Orbiter*

93. How many satellites make up the Global Positioning Satellites system?
    (a) 8
    (b) 16
    (c) 24
    (d) 32

94. What kind of sensors enable a satellite to keep track of missile launches on earth?
    (a) Ultraviolet sensor
    (b) Infrared sensor
    (c) X-ray sensor
    (d) Nuclear radiation sensor

95. Which satellite is likely to orbit the earth for the next 50, 000 years and will burn up in a spectacular show to announce our presence on the earth?
    (a) *Kalpana-1*
    (b) *Sputnik-2000*
    (c) *Kitsat-2*
    (d) *K.E.O.*

Spacecraft

96. How many spacecrafts were sent to study Halley's comet in 1985-86?
    (a) Two   (b) Four
    (c) Six   (d) Eight

97. Which is presently the most remote man-made object in the outer space?
    (a) *Pioneer-10*   (b) *Galileo Orbiter*
    (c) *Ulysses*   (d) *Pioneer-11*

98. What is the name of the robot craft sent to Mars to search for life in 1998?
    (a) *Discovery*   (b) *Sojouner*
    (c) *Viking-II*   (d) *Spacehab*

99. Which space vehicle is reusable?
    (a) *Atlantis*   (b) *Landsat*
    (c) *Salyut*   (d) *Saturn-5*

100. Which is the last manned spacecraft to have returned from the Moon?
    (a) *Lunik-21*   (b) *Apollo-14*
    (c) *Apollo-17*   (d) *Apollo-15*

101. Which spacecraft carried the record disc 'Sounds of Earth'?
    (a) *Pioneer-10*   (b) *Viking-II*
    (c) *Voyager-I*   (d) *Voyager-II*

102. Which celestial object was the object of study for the *Giotto* spaceprobe?
    (a) Saturn's rings   (b) Asteroid belt
    (c) Martian satellites (d) Halley's comet

103. What is *Progress* in the Russian space programme?
    (a) Robot ferry spacecraft
    (b) Astronomical satellite
    (c) Spy satellite
    (d) Manned ferry spacecraft

104. Which spacecraft carried the unmanned roving vehicle *Lunokhod* to the surface of the Moon?
    (a) *Luna-16*   (b) *Luna-15*
    (c) *Luna-17*   (d) *Luna-10*

105. Which space vehicle does not have a robot arm?
    (a) *Voyager-I*   (b) *Viking-II*
    (c) *Discovery*   (d) *INSAT-1C*

106. Which was the first spacecraft to land on the surface of the Moon?
    (a) *Ranger-6*   (b) *Lunik-9*
    (c) *Surveyor-1* (d) *Lunik-6*

107. Which were the first manned spacecraft to dock and transfer crew in space?
    (a) *Soyuz-2* and *Soyuz-3* (b) *Soyuz-4* and *Soyuz-5*
    (c) *Soyuz-6* and *Soyuz-7* (d) *Soyuz-8* and *Soyuz-9*

108. *Cassini* mission was sent to explore a planet, its rings and satellites. Which planet was it?
    (a) Uranus   (b) Pluto
    (c) Jupiter   (d) Saturn

109. Which country other than the superpowers is planning to send an exploratory spacecraft to Mars?
    (a) India   (b) Japan
    (c) China   (d) Germany

110. *Galileo* space probe was sent to a planet to study its ring system and satellites. Which planet was it?
    (a) Jupiter   (b) Saturn
    (c) Uranus   (d) Neptune

Space Shuttle

111. What type of launch vehicle does a space shuttle have?
    (a) One-stage   (b) Three-stage
    (c) Two-stage   (d) Four-stage

112. During which flight were communication satellites launched from a space shuttle for the first time?
    (a) Second   (b) Third
    (c) Fifth   (d) Sixth

113. When does a space shuttle lose radio contact with the ground station for about fifteen minutes ?
    (a) During lift-off   (b) In the orbit of earth
    (c) During landing   (d) On the runway

114. What is the uncommon name of the space shuttle's 'Cargo bay'?
    (a) Payload module   (b) Payload bay
    (c) Orbiter module   (d) Orbiter bay

115. Which was the first space shuttle flight launched at night and which also landed at night?
    (a) Second   (b) Fourth
    (c) Sixth   (d) Eighth

116. What is the major component of the US space shuttle likely to be absent in the Russian space shuttle?
    (a) Payload bay   (b) Air-brakes
    (c) Main engines   (d) Booster rockets

117. What is the most of the outer surface of the space shuttle covered with?
    (a) Solar cells   (b) Heat-resistant tiles
    (c) Lead shields   (d) Polyester material

118. During which space shuttle flight was *Spacelab* carried into space?
    (a) Ninth   (b) Seventh
    (c) Fifth   (d) Third

119. When does a space shuttle produce a 'sonic boom'?
    (a) Take-off   (b) Orbiting
    (c) Re-entry   (d) Landing

120. What kind of fuel initially lifts the space shuttle into space?
    (a) Liquid   (b) Gaseous
    (c) Solid   (d) Plasma

121. Long Duration Exposure Facility, a 12-sided cylinder housing a variety of experiments requiring long-term exposure to space, was launched by a space shuttle. Which was the mission?
    (a) Mission 51J   (b) Mission 61A
    (c) Mission 51L   (d) Mission 41C

122. Which space shuttle exploded on its launch?
    (a) *Enterprise*   (b) *Challenger*
    (c) *Columbia*   (d) *Discovery*

123. What are heat-resisting tiles covering the body of a space shuttle made of?
    (a) Carbon fibres   (b) Polymers
    (c) Ceramics   (d) All

124. Where is a 'Science laboratory' installed aboard a space shuttle for experiments in space?
- (a) Flight-deck
- (b) Mid-deck
- (c) Payload bay
- (d) Lower-deck

125. Where is a satellite kept aboard a space shuttle for launch into space?
- (a) Mid-deck
- (b) Payload bay
- (c) Flight-deck
- (d) Lockers

126. What does a space shuttle use for landing on the earth?
- (a) Rockets
- (b) Parachutes
- (c) Engines
- (d) Nothing

127. Which is the most critical phase of a space shuttle flight?
- (a) Lift-off
- (b) Orbital
- (c) Landing
- (d) All

128. To release heat generated aboard a space shuttle, doors of this are opened as soon as it enters space. Whose doors?
- (a) Payload bay
- (b) Flight deck
- (c) Air-lock
- (d) Mid-deck

129. Where are the thruster jets located on a space shuttle for manoeuvring in space?
   (a) Wings
   (b) Payload Bay
   (c) Nose
   (d) Tail

130. How many external tanks are used for launching a space shuttle into space?
   (a) One
   (b) Two
   (c) Three
   (d) Four

131. How many heat-resisting tiles cover the body of a space shuttle?
   (a) About 1, 000
   (b) About 21, 000
   (c) About 11, 000
   (d) About 31, 000

132. How many booster rockets carry a space shuttle into space?
   (a) One
   (b) Two
   (c) Three
   (d) Four

133. How many thruster jets are present on a space shuttle for manoeuvring in space?
   (a) 24
   (b) 34
   (c) 44
   (d) 54

134. How many types of engines a space shuttle has?
   (a) Two
   (b) Three
   (c) Four
   (d) Five

135. Which space shuttle recently exploded during its return to the earth?
   (a) *Atlantis*
   (b) *Endeavour*
   (c) *Columbia*
   (d) *Challenger*

136. What was the major trouble faced during the first orbital test flight of a space shuttle?
   (a) Solid booster leaked
   (b) Thermal tiles fell down
   (c) Landing delayed by weather
   (d) Flight curtailed by defective fuel cells

137. During which shuttle flight was the robotic Remote Manipulator System used for the first time?
   (a) First
   (b) Second
   (c) Third
   (d) Fourth

Space Vehicles

138. Which is this queer-looking spacecraft?

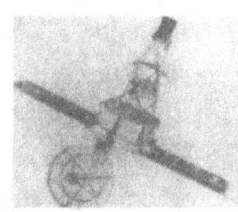

   - (a) *Mariner-I*
   - (b) *Pioneer-9*
   - (c) *Lunik-4*
   - (d) *Voyager-II*

139. Which is this famous space vehicle?

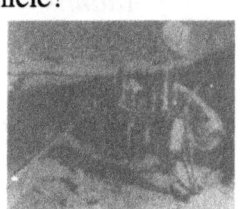

   - (a) *Viking* lander
   - (b) *Venera* lander
   - (c) *Ranger* lander
   - (d) *Lunik* lander

140. What object is this?

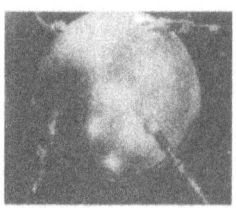

   - (a) *Echo-I*
   - (b) *Echo-II*
   - (c) *Sputnik-2*
   - (d) *Sputnik-I*

141. Which is this pioneer spacecraft?

   - (a) *Zond-2*
   - (b) *Vostok-1*
   - (c) *Apollo-4*
   - (d) *Surveyor-4*

142. What is this type of spacecraft?

   (a) *Apollo*
   (b) *Mercury*
   (c) *Soyuz*
   (d) *Gemini*

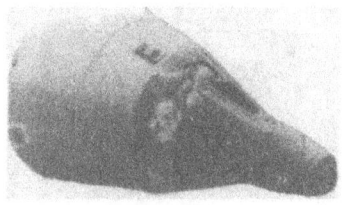

143. Which is this pioneer weather satellite?

   (a) *NOAA*
   (b) *Meteor*
   (c) *ITOS*
   (d) *TIROS*

144. Which is this satellite?

   (a) *INSAT-1B*
   (b) *Anik C-1*
   (c) *Seasat-1*
   (d) *Solar Max*

145. Which is this Indian satellite?

   (a) *Aryabhata-1*
   (b) *Rohini-1*
   (c) *Bhaskara-1*
   (d) *APPLE*

146. Which is this much talked about remote-sensing satellite?
- (a) *Landsat-2*
- (b) *Seasat-1*
- (c) *SPOT-1*
- (d) *ERS-1*

147. What is this odd-looking spacecraft?
- (a) *INSAT-3B*
- (b) *Space Shuttle*
- (c) *Seasat-2*
- (d) *Landsat-4*

148. This is an Indian satellite meant for scientific studies. Which is it?
- (a) *Aryabhata*
- (b) *APPLE*
- (c) *SROSS-C2*
- (d) *KITSAT-3*

149. Which is this Indian satellite with huge solar panels?
- (a) *Bhaskara*
- (b) *Rohini*
- (c) *INSAT-2D*
- (d) *Oceansat-1*

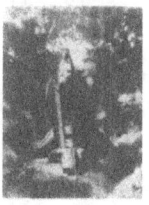

150. This is an astronomical observatory in space. What is it called?

(a) *Chandra X-ray Observatory*
(b) *COBE*
(c) *IRAS*
(d) *SROSS-C*

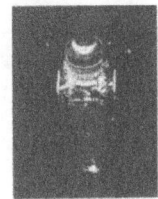

III

FLIGHTS

In Orbit

151. What is the Clarke orbit?
    (a) Geocentric orbit   (b) Geo-stationary orbit
    (c) Aero-centric orbit
    (d) Geo-synchronous orbit

152. When a rocket or spacecraft escapes from the gravitational pull of the earth it moves away from it in this curve. What is it?
    (a) Parabola   (b) Hyperbola
    (c) Straight line   (d) Ellipse

153. Which physical laws govern the operation of rockets?
    (a) Kepler's laws   (b) Newton's laws
    (c) Tsiolkovsky's laws   (d) All

154. What is the name of the ratio of the weight of the usable propellant to the final weight of the rocket or its stage after the engine is cut off?
    (a) Mach number
    (b) Stage ratio
    (c) Magic ratio
    (d) Tsiolkovsky number

155. Which orbit of a type of satellites is highly elliptical in shape?
    (a) Semi-synchronous
    (b) Geo-synchronous
    (c) Low earth
    (d) Molniya

156. Which is the point in the orbit of a spacecraft when it is nearest the sun?
    (a) Perihelion
    (b) Aphelion
    (c) Perigee
    (d) Apogee

157. What is the orbit that requires the minimum propellant consumption to transfer a spacecraft from one heavenly body to another?
    (a) Transfer orbit
    (b) Keplerian orbit
    (c) Intermediate orbit
    (d) Hohmann transfer

158. Which law gives the time an artificial satellite would take to go once around the earth if its distance from it (the earth) is known?
    (a) Newton's Second Law of Motion
    (b) Kepler's Third Planetary Law
    (c) Newton's Third Law of Motion
    (d) Kepler's First Planetary Law

159. What keeps an artificial satellite confined to its orbit around the earth?
    (a) Weight
    (b) Drag
    (c) Speed
    (d) Earth's rotation

160. Which is the point in the orbit of a spacecraft about the Moon that is farthest from its centre?
    (a) Perilune
    (b) Perigee
    (c) Apogee
    (d) Apolune

Space flight

161. What is the basic qualification required for be coming an astronaut?
    (a) Graduate
    (b) Flying experience
    (c) Sports person
    (d) All

162. What are the essential qualities required for becoming an astronaut?
    (a) Leadership/ team spirit
    (b) Communication skills
    (c) Medical fitness
    (d) All

163. What kind of training astronauts undergo before venturing into space?
    (a) Space/ anti-gravity simulation
    (b) Familiarity with spacecraft
    (c) Living in isolation and crises
    (d) All

164. When not in space, astronauts perform some regular duties like any office-worker. What is it?
   (a) Teaching/training astronauts
   (b) Transferring space spin-offs to the masses
   (c) Solving day-to-day problems encountered in space flights
   (d) All

165. What does an astronaut wear before he or she dons the spacesuit for moving about in space?
   (a) LCG   (b) CWG
   (c) TMG   (d) UCTA

166. Which waste item is discarded directly into space from a spacecraft?
   (a) Drink packs   (b) Urine
   (c) Faeces   (d) None of the above

167. Which call sign became popular during the US Apollo space missions?
   (a) Houston   (b) George
   (c) Goldstone   (d) Cape

168. Which is the star apart from the sun often used as a guide star by any spacecraft navigating in the solar system?
   (a) Sirius   (b) Canopus
   (c) Polaris   (d) Regulus

169. The flyby of a spacecraft across a planet is conducted using some force. What is it?
    (a) Magnetic field
    (b) Solar radiation pressure
    (c) Gravity
    (d) All

170. When a spaceeraft is carrying things not necessary for its operations, what is it known as?
    (a) Payload   (b) Overload
    (c) Extra load   (d) Load

171. Where does the 'Parking orbit' manoeuvre come into effect?
    (a) Satellite launch   (b) Spacecraft launch
    (c) Moon landing   (d) All

172. Why is the final stage of a Moon- or planet-bound spacecraft sterilised?
    (a) Mere hygiene   (b) As per convention
    (c) Avoid spread of germs to other heavenly bodies
    (d) All

173. While working in space, which among the following is a major hazard?
    (a) Losing balance   (b) Meteorite hit
    (c) Radiation   (d) Tumbling

174. Astronauts are reported to have seen 'Light flashes' during space flights. What are they due to?
    (a) Solar flares
    (b) Terrestrial magnetism
    (c) Cosmic rays
    (d) Pulsating stars

Inflight Health

175. What type of food is normally taken aboard a spacecraft because it has the minimum weight?
    (a) Dehydrated food   (b) Fried food
    (c) Vacuum-packed food (d) Baby food

176. Which syndrome has become a real psychological danger to astronauts during space travel?
    (a) Space adaptation   (b) Jet lag
    (c) Solipsism   (d) All

177. What drug do American astronauts often take one hour before the launch to combat space sickness?
    (a) Scopdex   (b) Cavinton
    (c) Campazine   (d) Valium

178. During long-term space missions, astronauts become sensitive to this. What is it?
    (a) Allergens   (b) Infections
    (c) Radiations   (d) All

179. Which is the most likely health bonus to an astronaut when he or she would stay for a very long period in space?
   (a) Increase in the muscle power
   (b) Slowing in the aging process
   (c) Lowering in the food requirements
   (d) Increase in the mental power

180. What is essential during a long stay in space?
   (a) Balanced diet   (b) Exercise
   (c) Both   (d) None

181. The inclusion of one chemical element in the diet of an astronaut is essential during long-term space missions. Which is it?
   (a) Iron   (b) Sodium
   (c) Zinc   (d) Calcium

182. What poses the most serious health problem during long-term space missions?
   (a) Altered metabolism   (b) Muscle deterioration
   (c) Bone deterioration   (d) Indigestion

183. Which is the first bodily complaint of an astronaut when he or she experiences space conditions?
   (a) Dizziness   (b) Vomiting
   (c) Backache   (d) All

184. What is banned during a stay in space today?
    (a) Tea   (b) Sex
    (c) Alcohol   (d) Ice-cream

185. When astronauts return from space, there appears a temporary change in their size. What is it?
    (a) Become shorter   (b) Become broader
    (c) Become taller   (d) Become fatter

Equipment

186. Which type of training simulator provides a weightless condition short of actual orbital flight, though for a very short time?
    (a) Neutral Buoyancy Simulator
    (b) Ballistic Trajectory
    (c) Horizontal Walking Device
    (d) Six Degrees of Operational Freedom Simulator

187. What kinds of tools are required for working in space?
    (a) Zero-reaction tools   (b) Zero-gravity tools
    (c) Zero-handling tools   (d) Ordinary tools

188. Which type of training simulator tests an astronaut's capacity to withstand higher g-forces?
    (a) Ballistic Trajectory
    (b) Six Degrees of Operational Freedom Simulator
    (c) Centrifuge
    (d) Multiple Axis Space Test Inertia Facility

189. Which device is used for transferring heat efficiently from one point to another in a spacecraft or satellite?
     (a) Heat shield
     (b) Refrigerator
     (c) Heat pipe
     (d) All

190. What is that a vacuum chamber, which simulates conditions of space, tests?
     (a) Spacecraft
     (b) Payload
     (c) Rocket
     (d) All

191. Which factors are taken into account while designing a spacesuit for survival in space?
     (a) Gravity
     (b) Temperature
     (c) Pressure
     (d) Radiation

192. Which was the source of electricity aboard *Voyager I* and *II* that explored the outer regions of the solar system?
     (a) Solar cell
     (b) Radioisotope thermoelectric generator
     (c) MHD generator
     (d) Thermoelectric generator

193. What is used by a spacecraft or satellite to boost itself from a parking orbit to a higher orbit?
     (a) Apogee motor
     (b) Booster engine
     (c) Cryogenic engine
     (d) All

194. Which is the electromechanical device that supplies and transmits energy to control the operation of other devices aboard a spacecraft?
    (a) Robot
    (b) Servomechanism
    (c) Sensor
    (d) All

195. Which type of antenna is commonly used in satellite earth stations?
    (a) Horn-parabolic antenna
    (b) Yagi antenna
    (c) Cassegrain two-mirror antenna
    (d) All

Instruments

196. Which is the instrument that maintains distance between a spacecraft and the surface of the celestial body in its neighbourhood?
    (a) Altimeter
    (b) Tachometer
    (c) Radiometer
    (d) Anemometer

197. What is the main component of the inertial guidance unit in rockets and spacecraft?
    (a) Barometer
    (b) Sextant
    (c) Accelerometer
    (d) Gyroscope

198. Which type of satellites contain transponders?
    (a) Spy satellites
    (b) Remote sensing satellites
    (c) Communication satellites (d) All

199. Which instrument is an essential part of an instrument package on another planet?
    (a) Telescope   (b) Anemometer
    (c) Microscope   (d) All

200. Which electronic instrument is used to measure very high temperatures, above 600 degree C, in space?
    (a) Thermistor   (b) Pyrometer
    (c) Thermometer   (d) Thermostat

201. What is used aboard a spacecraft to determine its bearings in space?
    (a) Astrograph   (b) Astrolabe
    (c) Star sensor   (d) Sextant

202. Which instrument is the heart and soul of a weather satellite?
    (a) Gas laser   (b) Radiometer
    (c) Geiger counter   (d) Photometer

203. Which instrument was placed on the surface of the Moon when the first men landed on it?
    (a) Laser ranging retro-reflector
    (b) Seismometer
    (c) Windowshade   (d) All
204. Which instrument aboard a space probe measures the strength of a heavenly body's magnetic field?
    (a) Magnetograph   (b) Magnetic balance
    (c) Magnetometer   (d) All

205. What is the main instrument aboard an earth survey satellite such as *Landsat*?
    (a) Laser ranger   (b) Thematic mapper
    (c) Multi-spectral scanner(d) Side-borne radar

IV

NAMES AND SUBJECTS

Names

206. Which space shuttle is named after the spaceship in the *Star Trek* TV serial?
    (a) *Enterprise*   (b) *Columbus*
    (c) *Discovery*   (d) *Atlantis*

207. What is the name of Japan's first artificial satellite?
    (a) *Offeq*   (b) *Ajisai*
    (c) *Ohsumi*   (d) *Fuji*

208. What was the name of satellite conceived on paper in the true modern sense?
    (a) *Vanguard*   (b) *Explorer*
    (c) *MOUSE*   (d) *Sputnik*

209. Which space probe is named after a famous Italian artist?
    (a) *HEAO*   (b) *Giotto*
    (c) *Hipparcos*   (d) *Galileo*

210. Which satellite meant for studying X-ray sources and cosmic rays was renamed the Einstein Observatory?
    (a) *HEAO-1*   (b) *HEAO-2*
    (c) *HEAO-3*   (d) *Ariel-5*

211. What was the name of the German V-2 (VfR) rocket when it was first tested?
    (a) *Repulsor*   (b) *Cavorite*
    (c) *Mirak*   (d) *Winkler*

212. What other uncommon name is a space shuttle called by?
    (a) OTV   (b) OMV
    (c) STS   (d) SPAS

213. Which series of satellites was earlier known as the 'Earth Resources Technology Satellite'?
    (a) *Landsat*   (b) *SPOT*
    (c) *GEOS*   (d) *Cosmos*

214. Which satellite for astronomical studies was named Copernicus after that great pioneering astronomer?
    (a) *Orbiting Astronomical Observatory-3*
    (b) *Orbiting Astronomical Observatory-2*
    (c) *International Ultraviolet Explorer*
    (d) *International Solar Polar Mission*

215. Which country's rocket launcher is named after a historic event?
    (a) Russia   (b) France
    (c) China   (d) India

216. Which Indian series of satellites has now been named *Kalpana* in honour of the astronaut?
    (a) *Metsat*   (b) *Oceansat*
    (c) *GSAT*   (d) *INSAT*

Space Parlance

217. 'Space walk radio' is the radio carried by an astronaut during his stay in space. What is its purpose?
    (a) Keep in touch with other spacecraft
    (b) Provide information about the astronaut's heart-beat and other bodily functions
    (c) Alert an astronaut if the life-support systems are running low
    (d) All

218. Who is 'Payload Specialist' during a space shuttle flight?
    (a) Non-pilot astronaut
    (b) Astronaut who looks after a particular experiment
    (c) Astronaut who looks after a particular payload
    (d) All

219. What is the technical term for a 'spacesuit'?
    (a) Non-vehicular manoeuvre unit
    (b) Personal mobility unit
    (c) Extravehicular mobility unit
    (d) None of the above

220. 'Space medicine' is a drug. What is it?
    (a) Administered for the well-being of astronauts during space flights
    (b) Developed in space
    (c) Tested in the conditions of space
    (d) All

221. What is a 'Selenoid'?
    (a) A spacecraft in lunar orbit
    (b) A spacecraft in solar orbit
    (c) An astronaut in lunar orbit
    (d) An astronaut in solar orbit

222. What is the technical term for 'space walking'?
   (a) Extraspace manoeuvre
   (b) Extravehicular activity
   (c) Space transportation
   (d) Non-vehicular manoeuvre

223. Who is a 'Spacenik'?
   (a) Recently returned from the space
   (b) Enthusiastic about space activities
   (c) Loves criticising space activities
   (d) Visited space several times

224. What is a 'module' of a spacecraft?
   (a) A self-contained unit   (b) Common unit
   (c) Crew quarters   (d) Control unit

225. Who is a 'Mission Specialist' abroad a space shuttle?
   (a) Non-pilot astronaut
   (b) Pilot-astronaut
   (c) Chief astronaut
   (d) Astronaut who looks after a laboratory

226. What is the person who remotely controls a
   spacecraft from an earth station known as?
   (a) Navigator   (b) Controller
   (c) Remote controller (d) Commander

227. Who is a 'Flight Engineer' abroad a space shuttle?
   (a) Maintains engineering aspects of the shuttle
   (b) Flies the shuttle
   (c) Navigates the shuttle
   (d) Designs the shuttle

228. Who is the 'Commander' of a space shuttle?
   (a) An experienced astronaut
   (b) An experienced pilot
   (c) An experienced engineer
   (d) An experienced navigator

Subjects

229. What is known as the science and technology of space flight?
   (a) Cosmonautics   (b) Aeronautics
   (c) Astronautics   (d) Astro-dynamics

230. Which subject is likely to play a major role in the future space missions?
   (a) Cybernetics   (b) Telematics
   (c) Bioastronautics   (d) Robotics

231. What is the study of living organisms in space called?
   (a) Bioastronautics   (b) Cybernetics
   (c) Space medicine   (d) Cryogenics

232. What is the transmission of measurements by radio made at a distance in space known as?
   (a) Radar   (b) Telegraphy
   (c) Interferometry   (d) Telemetry

233. What is the study of the nature of planets of the solar system called?
   (a) Selenography   (b) Planetology
   (c) Planetography   (d) Cosmology

234. What is obtaining information about distant objects using some type of instruments known as?
   (a) Meterology   (b) Radiometry
   (c) Aerography   (d) Remote sensing

235. What is the study of motion of gases at high velocities required for space flight called?
   (a) Aerodynamics   (b) Gas Dynamics
   (c) Aeroballistics   (d) Kinetics

236. What is the remote measurement of life functions of animals and man using radio waves known as?
   (a) Telemetry   (b) Biotelemetry
   (c) Space medicine   (d) Remote sensing

237. What is the study of how artificial satellites, space craft, and heavenly bodies move through space under the influence of gravitational fields called?
   (a) Mechanics   (b) Astrometry
   (c) Celestial Mechanics (d) Cosmonautics

238. What is the study of physics of the earth, its atmosphere, and neighbouring space called?
   (a) Geology   (b) Geomagnetism
   (c) Geophysics   (d) Meteorology

Associations

239. What is Complex 39 associated with?
   (a) Future lunar base   (b) Space station
   (c) Earth station   (d) Launch site

240. What is the term 'Skirt' associated with?
   (a) Satellite   (b) Rocket
   (c) Space shuttle   (d) Space probe

241. What is the term 'Hot test' associated with?
   (a) Flight test   (b) Shield test
   (c) Captive test   (d) Instrumentation test

242. What is the term 'Flight deck' associated with?
   (a) Satellite   (b) Space shuttle
   (c) Rocket   (d) Lander

243. What is the term 'Eyeballs in, eyeballs out' concerned with?
   (a) Tumbling in space   (b) Leaving the air-lock
   (c) Rocket firing   (d) Space shuttle roll

244. What is the term 'ASAT' associated with?
   (a) Rocket   (b) Missile
   (c) Spacecraft   (d) Satellite

245. What is the term 'Umbilical' concerned with?
   (a) Life-support system   (b) Spacesuit
   (c) Spacecraft   (d) All

246. What is the 'Mobile launch platform' associated with?
   (a) Space Shuttle   (b) *Saturn-5*
   (c) Space station   (d) Spacelab

247. What is the term 'Abort' associated with?
   (a) Orbit   (b) Landing
   (c) Launch   (d) Boost

248. What is a 'Launch window' associated with?
   (a) Hyperspace   (b) Time interval
   (c) Temperature gradient (d) Gravity

V

DATES

Turning Points

249. When were rockets used for the first time for conducting astronomical studies?
    (a) 1952 (b) 1949
    (c) 1822 (d) 1907

250. When did Robert Goddard launch the first liquid-propelled rocket?
    (a) 1957 (b) 1890
    (c) 1926 (d) 1945

251. When was the US National Aeronautics and Space Administration founded?
    (a) 1962 (b) 1948
    (c) 1952 (d) 1958

252. When were the V-2 bomb-carrying rockets launched against London in retaliation for the Allied air attack on Germany?
   (a) 1941
   (b) 1942
   (c) 1943
   (d) 1944

253. When was the 'Society for Space Travel' founded by a group of German scientists?
   (a) 1918
   (b) 1927
   (c) 1932
   (d) 1942

254. When was the first anti-satellite missile successfully launched by the US Air Force?
   (a) 1982
   (b) 1983
   (c) 1984
   (d) 1985

255. When did Tippu Sultan fight the battle against the British might in which he used rockets on Indian soil for the first time?
   (a) 1792
   (b) 1780
   (c) 1789
   (d) 1797

256. When did three Russian spacecrafts dock together in space forming a spacecraft complex?
   (a) 1976
   (b) 1977
   (c) 1978
   (d) 1979

257. When was the Committee on Space Research (COSPAR) for conducting space research on an international scale with the use of rockets and satellites founded?
    (a) 1952   (b) 1954
    (c) 1958   (d) 1960

258. When did Arthur C. Clarke propose the idea of geo-synchronous satellites for intercontinental communications?
    (a) 1945   (b) 1932
    (c) 1953   (d) 1964

259. When was the European Space Agency meant to build launchers and spacecraft under a co-operative effort of European countries established?
    (a) 1975   (b) 1959
    (c) 1967   (d) 1982

Significant Dates

260. When did a US Space Shuttle blow apart during its launch?
    (a) 1986   (b) 1982
    (c) 1983   (d) 1985

261. When was the first *Soyuz* spacecraft launched?
    (a) 1982   (b) 1958
    (c) 1974   (d) 1967

262. In which year did a US space station fall down to the earth like a meteor over the Indian Ocean?
    (a) 1979   (b) 1975
    (c) 1982   (d) 1980

263. When were the *Voyager* space probes launched to Jupiter and the outer planets?
    (a) 1977   (b) 1972
    (c) 1975   (d) 1976

264. When was the civilian space agency *Glavkosmos* established in the erstwhile USSR to manage space science, space applications and co-operative international space programmes?
    (a) 1989   (b) 1985
    (c) 1990   (d) 1986

265. When was the Woomera rocket range in South Australia re-opened for scientific research by sounding rockets?
    (a) 1987   (b) 1967
    (c) 1957   (d) 1977

266. In which year were the three US *Skylabs* launched?
    (a) 1964   (b) 1970
    (c) 1976   (d) 1973

267. When was the first *Landsat*, the US earth-survey satellite, launched?
    (a) 1962   (b) 1972
    (c) 1982   (d) 1986

268. Which day is celebrated as the 'Cosmonautics Day' in Russia?
    (a) October 4   (b) June 16
    (c) November 3   (d) April 12

269. When was the world's first telephone call made from an aeroplane to the ground via a satellite?
    (a) 1962   (b) 1987
    (c) 1975   (d) 1990

270. When was the Russian *Mir* space station with the record of longest stay in space launched?
    (a) 1976   (b) 1986
    (c) 1981   (d) 1971

271. When was the Cosmic Background Explorer satellite (COBE) to study radiation remnants of the early universe launched?
    (a) 1989   (b) 1999
    (c) 1969   (d) 1979

272. When did a Space Shuttle blow up while returning from space?
    (a) 2000   (b) 2001
    (c) 2002   (d) 2003

VI

SOCIETIES, AWARDS AND PROJECTS

Space Bodies

273. Which body founded the Committee on Space Research (COSPAR) for conducting space research on an international scale?
    (a) International Astronautical Federation
    (b) International Council of Scientific Unions
    (c) International Union of Geodesy and Geophysics
    (d) International Telecommunications Union

274. Which space travel society become more popular as 'VfR' all over the world?
    (a) British Interplanetary Society
    (b) Society for Space Travel
    (c) American Rocket Society
    (d) Group for Investigation of Reaction Motion

275. Which body built the re-usable space laboratory
    Spacelab for space shuttle flights?
    (a) European Space Agency
    (b) Kagoshima Space Center
    (c) National Space Development Agency
    (d) Centre National d'Etudes Spatiales

276. Where was the first society for space travel founded?
    (a) Germany   (b) USA
    (c) Italy   (d) Russia.

277. Which body has set up Office of Exploration
    with the goal to expand human presence beyond
    the earth?
    (a) ESA   (b) BNSC
    (c) NASA   (d) NASDA

278. Where is the headquarters of the British Interp-
    lanetary Society, which promotes the exploration and
    use of space, located?
    (a) London   (b) Cambridge
    (c) Glasgow   (d)   Oxford

279. Which organisation flies experimental packages in
    the payload bay of the US Space Shuttle?
    (a) MAUS   (b) SPAS
    (c) OSTA
    (d) No separate organisation exists

280. Which organisation deals with the space affairs of Japan?
   - (a) CNES
   - (b) ISRO
   - (c) ISAS
   - (d) NASDA

281. Which organisation provides worldwide communication and other services via satellites to ships and offshore platforms?
   - (a) INTELSAT
   - (b) INMARSAT
   - (c) ESA
   - (d) RADARSAT

282. Which American body is devoted to encouraging participation of women in space exploration?
   - (a) National Space Club
   - (b) Hypatia Cluster
   - (c) National Space Institute
   - (d) Spaceweek

283. The sole aim of the American L-5 Society is to establish this. What is it?
   - (a) A space station
   - (b) A lunar colony
   - (c) A space colony
   - (d) All

284. Which body is acquainting school children with various aspects of space travel for the upcoming International Space Station ?
   - (a) International Space School Foundation
   - (b) National Space Institute
   - (c) Society for Space Travel
   - (d) The Planetary Society

285. Where is the NASA's astronaut training centre?
    (a) Kennedy Space Center
    (b) Johnson Space Center
    (c) Goddard Spaceflight Center
    (d) Ames Research Center

Awards

286. Which body awards the International Aeronautical Federation Gold Space Medal to an astronaut for outstanding achievements in space?
    (a) Royal Aeronautical Society
    (b) European Space Agency
    (c) Federation Aeronautique Internationale
    (d) Smithsonian Institution

287. Which body awards the Hoyt S. Vandenburg Award for contributions to aerospace education?
    (a) American Institute of Aeronautics and Aerospace
    (b) US Air Force Association
    (c) Canadian Aeronautics and Space Institution
    (d) Royal Aeronautical Society

288. Which body gives the Space Science Award to an individual for conducting notable studies of space?
    (a) Indian Space Research Organisation
    (b) British Interplanetary Society
    (c) US National Academy of Sciences
    (d) American Institute of Aeronautics ad Astronautics

289. Which body gives the Wyld Propulsion Award to an individual for development and application of rocket propulsion systems?
    (a) European Space Agency
    (b) American Institute of Aeronautics and Astronautics
    (c) British Interplanetary Society
    (d) USSR Academy of Sciences

290. Which body gives the Halley Space Flight Award to an astronaut or test flight personnel for the advancement of art, science, or technology of astronautics?
    (a) National Aeronautics and Space Administration
    (b) European Space Agency
    (c) American Institute of Aeronautics and Astronautics
    (d) USSR Academy of Sciences

291. Which body awards the Gagarin Medal to a space person for making outstanding contributions to the peaceful conquest of space?
    (a) Federation Aeronautique Internationale
    (b) International Astronautical Federation
    (c) International Peace Foundation
    (d) International Union of Scientific Workers

292. Which body awards the Korolev Medal for out standing achievements in rocket engineering and space flights?
    (a) USSR Academy of Sciences
    (b) International Academy of Astronautics
    (c) International Astronautical Federation
    (d) US National Academy of Sciences

293. Which body gives the Goddard Astronautics Award to an individual for notable contributions to astronautics?
    (a) American Institute of Aeronautics and Astronautics
    (b) National Aeronautics and Space Administration
    (c) National Space Development Agency
    (d) U. S. National Academy of Sciences

294. Which body awards the Cosmos Medal for out
standing contributions in space exploration?
   (a) International Astronautical Federation
   (b) International Academy of Astronautics
   (c) American Rocket Society
   (d) International Institute of Space Law

295. Which space body gives the Zeldovich Award for
contributions to ionospheric physics?
   (a) COSPAR   (b) CNES
   (c) ESSA   (d) NASDA

Programmes and Projects

296. Which was the pioneering American project aimed
at launching man into an orbit of the earth and re-
cover both man and spacecraft?
   (a) Gemini   (b) Mariner
   (c) Ranger   (d) Mercury

297. Which type of futuristic craft is the goal of the
U.S. programme, called the National Aerospace
Plane?
   (a) *HOTOL*   (b) *Sanger*
   (c) *Hermes*   (d) *X-30*

298. What is the Sentinel Project concerned with?
  (a) Shooting meteors from space.
  (b) Searching for intelligence in the universe.
  (c) Searching for an alien spaceship in the solar system.
  (d) Keeping an eye on anti-satellite weapons.

299. Which American space programme was aimed at taking close-up photographs of the Moon, among other things?
  (a) *Apollo*   (b) *Gemini*
  (c) *Ranger*   (d) *Viking*

300. What does the 'Star Wars' programme essentially centred on?
  (a) Nuclear weapon-equipped satellites
  (b) Laser-equipped satellites
  (c) Infrared-equipped spy satellites
  (d) Laser-equipped ground-based weapons

301. What was the aim of the US Orion Project?
  (a) To use atomic energy for rocket propulsion.
  (b) To use solar energy for rocket propulsion.
  (c) To design an interplanetary spaceship.
  (d) To design a space station.

302. Which space programme had regularly conducted 'docking' manoeuvres between two spacecrafts in space?
   (a) Soyuz   (b) Apollo
   (c) Gemini   (d) Cosmos

303. Which was the first US space programme with the Moon as its prime goal?
   (a) Surveyor   (b) Lunik
   (c) Apollo   (d) Ranger

304. Which space organisation has the scientific programme *Horizon 2000*?
   (a) NASA   (b) ESA
   (c) ISRO   (d) ISAS

305. Project Deadalus is a detailed engineering report on how to build this. What is it?
   (a) A manned space station
   (b) A colony on the Moon
   (c) A spaceport
   (d) An unmanned spaceship for exploring the neighbouring stars

VII

LITERATURE AND QUOTES

Literature and Language

306. Who composed *The Star-Spangled Banner* which included the phrase '... the rocket's red glare'?
    (a) Francis Scott Key
    (b) Walt Whitman
    (c) C.S. Lewis
    (d) Dylan Thomas

307. Who wrote the following perceptive lines which have come true about our space programmes?
    'We shall not cease from exploration
    And the end of all our exploring
    Will be to arrive where we started
    And know the place for the first time.'
    (a) S. T. Coleridge   (b) T. S. Eliot
    (c) Walt Whitman   (d) Alfred Tennyson

308. Who wrote the novel *Space* which centres on the lives of an astronaut, a rocket engineer, an astronomer, and a scientist?
    - (a) Saul Bellow
    - (b) James A. Michener
    - (c) Irving Stone
    - (d) Irving Wallace

309. Whose poem was the first to be sent up into space, inscribed on the instrument panel of the satellite *Traac* space probe?
    - (a) Walt Whitman
    - (b) Thomas G. Bergin
    - (c) T. S. Eliot
    - (d) S. T. Coleridge

310. Who wrote these poetic lines?
    'There is more challenge in each square block of city slum than all the galaxy.
    Between Brother and Brother, more awful distance, Than the long boulevard of lonely space.
    It will be written that in 1969, primitive man canned himself
    And catapulted through the void,
    While hunger, hate and sickness stalked his earth;
    Choosing not to try for Heaven, just the Moon'?
    - (a) Rabindranath Tagore
    - (b) Charles Joelson
    - (c) Piet Hein
    - (d) Anonymous

311. Which medieval poet wrote novels describing several ways of reaching the sun and the Moon?
   (a) Francois de Malherbe (b) John Milton
   (c) George Herbert
   (d) Savinien Cyrano de Bergerac

312. What is the slang for a rocket or a satellite?
   (a) Mouse   (b) Kite
   (c) Bat   (d) Bird

313. Which English poet thought that it was possible to use steam power to reach the Moon?
   (a) William Blake   (b) P. B. Shelley
   (c) Alfred Tennyson   (d) Lord Byron

314. Which novel of French writer Voltaire involves interplanetary wanderings of a Saturnian?
   (a) *Candide*   (b) *Micromegas*
   (c) *Zadig*
   (d) No such novel was written

Science Fiction

315. Which eminent astronomer wrote the authentic science fiction *Somnium* about a journey to the Moon in a dream?
   (a) Johannes Hevelius   (b) Tycho Brahe
   (c) Johann Kepler   (d) G. P. Kuiper

316. Which writer used a storm to carry a ship to the Moon?
    (a) A. K. Firdausi   (b) F. Godwin
    (c) Lucian of Samosata   (d) Voltaire

317. Who wrote the *Gun Club* series of novels in which heroes were sent to the Moon in a cannon shell?
    (a) F. Godwin   (b) Edger Allan Poe
    (c) Alexandre Dumas   (d) Jules Verne

318. Which science fiction film was banned from screening in Germany during World War II by Adolf Hitler because it contained space travel?
    (a) *The First Men in the Moon*
    (b) *The Last Man on Earth*
    (c) *Forbidden Planet*
    (d) *Woman on the Moon*

319. Who wrote the popular science fiction *On Two Planets* which showed how Martians developed their rockets and reached the earth?
    (a) Ray Bradbury   (b) H. G. Wells
    (c) Kurt Lasswitz   (d) Arthur C. Clarke

320. Which writer was the first to make suggestion of the reaction principle as a means of space travel in his science fiction?
    (a) K. E. Tsiolkovsky   (b) Kurt Lasswitz
    (c) Achille Eyraud   (d) H. G. Wells

321. Who wrote the science fiction containing for the first time the idea of an artificial satellite of earth?
    (a) Jules Verne   (b) H. G. Wells
    (c) K. E. Tsiolkovsky
    (d) Edward Everett Hale

322. Which science fiction depicts an encounter in space between human beings and creatures living on a neutron star?
    (a) *The Song of Earth*   (b) *Mission of Gravity*
    (c) *Dragon's Egg*   (d) *Neutron Star*

323. Which space pioneer wrote the science fiction *Outside the Earth*?
    (a) K. E. Tsiolkovsky   (b) Hermann Ganswindt
    (c) Reinhold Tiling   (d) Max Valier

324. Which writer invented an anti-gravity material 'Cavorite' to lift his spaceship from the earth for journey to the Moon?
    (a) H. G. Wells   (b) Jules Verne
    (c) K. E. Tsiolkovsky   (d) Kurt Lasswitz

325. Who wrote a series of realistic novels depicting life of human colonists on Mars?
    (a) William Gibson
    (b) Kim Stanley Robinson
    (c) Greg Bear   (d) Bruce Sterling

326. Which science fictional movie showed a friendly and lovable alien being?
   (a) *E. T.*
   (b) *Terminator*
   (c) *Predator*
   (d) *Mars Attacks*

327. Which science fictional movie depicted a hostile alien trying to conquer mankind?
   (a) *Independence Day*
   (b) *Invasion of the Body Snatchers*
   (c) *Return of the Jedi*
   (d) *Matrix*

328. Which science fiction film repeatedly emphasised the 'prime directive' not to contaminate alien societies with terrestrial biology?
   (a) *Star Wars*
   (b) *Star Trek*
   (c) *Jurassic Park*
   (d) All

329. Who wrote a series of realistic novels of space travel, of which the most popular is *2001: A Space Odyssey*?
   (a) Ray Bradbury
   (b) Arthur C. Clarke
   (c) Isaac Asimov
   (d) Stanislaw Lem

Quotations

330. Which modern philosopher remarked, 'Space travel … is an extravagant feat of technological exhibitionism'?
   (a) Albert Schweitzer
   (b) M. K. Gandhi
   (c) Lewis Mumford
   (d) Karl Popper

331. Which space-farer said, 'Space is a double loneliness'?
    (a) Valdimir Lyakhov
    (b) Gerald Carr
    (c) Michael Collins
    (d) Aleksandr Aleksandrov

332. Who said, 'Space is important because there are things we can do better in space, and other things we can't do at all on earth'?
    (a) Micheal Sander   (b) Richard Nixon
    (c) Indira Gandhi   (d) John Kulpa Jr

333. When did Bruce McCandless say the following words, 'That may have been one small step for Neil, but it was a heck of a big leap for me'?
    (a) Landing on Mercury
    (b) Moving in space without a tether
    (c) Walking in space
    (d) None of the above

334. Who said about the German V-2 rocket: 'It was very successful, but it fell on the wrong planet?
    (a) Winston Churchill   (b) Arthur C. Clarke
    (c) Werner von Braun   (d) John von Neumann

335. Which medieval astronomer talked about space travel thus, 'Let us create vessels and sails adjusted to the heavenly ether, and there will be plenty of peopl unafraid of the empty wastes'?
   (a) Jean Richter   (b) Olaus Roemer
   (c) Henry Gellibrand   (d) Johann Kepler

336. Who remarked, 'Space isn't remote at all. It's only an hour's drive away if your car could go straight upwards'?
   (a) Isaac Asimov   (b) Arthur C. Clarke
   (c) Willy Ley   (d) Fred Hoyle

337. Which astronaut remarked, 'People think we're tossed into centrifuges, dunked into water and thrown out of planes in this work. But it's not always exciting. We sit behind desks and go to meetings mostly'?
   (a) Alan Bean   (b) Robert Stewart
   (c) Sally Ride   (d) Rhea Seddon

338. Which Indian space scientist said, 'The question is not whether a developing country like ours should adopt space technology; the question is whether we can afford to ignore it'?
   (a) Vikram Sarabhai   (b) U. R. Rao
   (c) K. Kasturirangan   (d) Satish Dhawan

339. Which astronaut sent this message to students, 'The path from dreams to success does exist. May you have the vision to find it, the courage to get on to it, and the perseverance to follow it'?
   (a) Rick Husband   (b) Kalpana Chawla
   (c) Ilan Ramon   (d) Laurel Clark

340. Which astronaut said, 'The vast loneliness of the Moon ... makes you realise just what you have back there on earth'?
   (a) Jim Lovell   (b) Frank Borman
   (c) Valdmir Remek   (d) Sally Ride

341. Which physicist said, 'Empty space is not empty. It is the seat of the most violent physics'?
   (a) P. A. M. Dirac   (b) Vikram Sarabhai
   (c) John Wheeler   (d) Albert Einstein

342. Which politician and statesman said, 'The stone age may return on the gleaming wings of fire'?
   (a) Jawahar Lal Nehru   (b) Winston Churchill
   (c) Thomas Paine   (d) Joseph Stalin

343. Which rocket pioneer had said, 'I represent the revolutionary spirit of science and technology'?
   (a) K. E. Tsiolkovsky   (b) Hermann Oberth
   (c) Werner von Braun   (d) Robert Goddard

344. Who said, 'Space is inherently a global technology'?
    (a) Vannevar Bush
    (b) R. Buckminster Fuller
    (c) Harvey Brooks   (d) U. R. Rao

345. Who said, 'Space is a stage upon which international competition takes place, national technology is verified, and national values are affirmed'?
    (a) George Bush   (b) Alcestis R. Oberg
    (c) Satish Dhawan   (d) Hermann Bondi

346. Who said, 'Space is the hole that we are in'?
    (a) John Wheeler   (b) James van Allen
    (c) Stewart Brand   (d) Ray Bradbury

347. Who said some time ago, 'We're about to enter the age of flight, before we've not even developed chair that a man can sit on comfortably'?
    (a) Charlie Chaplin   (b) M. Freehill
    (c) Bob Hope   (d) Woody Allen

348. Who said, 'Space (travel) for a time reflected our past greatness, as it now reflects confusion and lack of purpose'?
    (a) Isaac Asimov   (b) Willy Ley
    (c) Bruce Murray   (d) Carl Sagan

349. Who said, 'Space manufacturing is a solution looking for a problem'?
    (a) Brahm Prakash
    (b) R. Buckminster Fuller
    (c) Gerard K. O'Neill
    (d) Max Lerner

350. Who said, 'One of the most important effects of human habitation in space will be to make all of us re-examine the whole idea: what is the meaning of territory'?
    (a) Frank Drake   (b) Margaret Mead
    (c) Gerard K. O'Neill   (d) Jim Irwin

351. Which rocket pioneer said, 'It is impossible to say what is impossible ; yesterday's dreams are today's hopes and tomorrow's reality'?
    (a) Hermann Oberth   (b) Robert Goddard
    (c) Krafte Ehricke   (d) Werner von Braun

352. Which scientist remarked, 'When mankind moves out from earth into space, we carry out problems with us'?
    (a) U. R. Rao   (b) James Watson
    (c) George Wald   (d) Freeman Dyson

353. Which politician once remarked, 'Today, man is more obsessed by the mysteries of outer space than by the composition of the earth he walks on, the ocean he sails, and the mountain he climbs"?
    (a) Richard Nixon   (b) Julius Nyerere
    (c) Indira Gandhi   (d) John F. Kennedy

354. Which astronaut said, 'One can imagine how risky it is to be an astronaut when even the fire brigade is five miles away from the launch site'?
    (a) Frank Borman
    (b) Valentina Tereshkova
    (c) John Glenn   (d) Mary Cleave

355. Which astronaut said, 'Fastening things together in space is easy – but they'll have to invent a more comfortable suit to wear'?
    (a) Frank Borman
    (b) Charles 'Pete' Conrad Jr
    (c) John Glenn   (d) Rick Husband

356. Which astronaut said, 'The astronaut's job requires a technical background and a strong desire... to go out in the blue wonder'?
    (a) Sally Ride   (b) Kalpana Chawla
    (c) Catherine Coleman   (d) Mary L. Cleave

VIII

PRINTED LITERATURE

Books and Journals

357. Who wrote the classic on military rockets *A Concise Account on the Origin and Progress of the Rocket System*?
    (a) Alexander D. Zasyadko
    (b) William Congreve
    (c) William Moore
    (d) Thomas Desaguliers

358. Which rocket pioneer wrote *The Seventh Continent* describing the colonisation and industrialisation of the Moon?
    (a) Krafte Ehricke   (b) K. E. Tsiolkovsky
    (c) Hermann Ganswindt
    (d) Yuri Kondratyuk

359. Where was the first book on fire-arrow or rocket technology *Complete Compendium of Military Classics* written?
   (a) UK   (b) India
   (c) China   (d) Greece

360. Which body publishes the semi-popular journal on astronautics *Spaceflight*?
   (a) European Space Agency
   (b) British Interplanetary Society
   (c) National Aeronautics and Space Administration
   (d) Jet Propulsion Laboratory

361. Who wrote *The Right Stuff,* a collection of biographies of US astronauts?
   (a) Tom Wolfe   (b) Bill Yenne
   (c) Willy Ley   (d) Andrew Wilson

362. Which rocket pioneer wrote *To Those Who Will Read in Order to Build* explaining the basic problems of space flight?
   (a) Sergei P. Korolev
   (b) Yuri Kondratyuk
   (c) Nikolai Rynin
   (d) Eugene Sanger

363. Which society brought out the first magazine *The Rocket* exclusively devoted to space travel?
   (a) Society for Space Travel
   (b) Society for Studying Interplanetary Travel
   (c) American Rocket Society
   (d) British Interplanetary Society

364. Which woman astronaut wrote her autobiography *Woman Into Space*?
   (a) Jerrie Cobb   (b) Mary Cleave
   (c) Valentina Tereshkova (d) Judith Resnik

365. Which body publishes the monthly *Aeronautics and Astronautics* on aerospace and space affairs of the world?
   (a) American Astronautical Society
   (b) British Interplanetary Society
   (c) American Society for Aerospace Education
   (d) American Institute of Aeronautics and Astronautics

366. Who wrote the classic *The High Frontier* about the next step of man into space?
   (a) George S. Robinson (b) Thomas Karas
   (c) J. E. Pournelle   (d) Gerard K. O'Neill

367. Which astronaut wrote *Return to Earth* in which he describes the mental trauma he underwent after attaining his life's goal – the Moon?
    (a) Harrison Schmitt   (b) Ronald E. Evans
    (c) Edwin E. Aldrin   (d) David Scott

368. Which American body publishes the magazine *Space World* that gives space news, among other things?
    (a) National Space Club
    (b) Space Studies Institute
    (c) National Space Institute
    (d) Universities Space Research Association

369. Which space pioneer's book *The Ultimate Migration* containing the idea of migration of mankind to another star was published years later?
    (a) K. E. Tsiolkovsky
    (b) Hermann Ganswindt
    (c) Robert H. Goddard   (d) Hermann Oberth

370. Who wrote *Outer Space – Battlefield of the Future* giving in detail the military use of space?
    (a) Bhupendra M. Jasani
    (b) Frank Barnaby
    (c) P. J. Klass
    (d) Kenneth Gatland

371. Which Indian space pioneer's autobiography is
Wings of Fire?
   (a) Satish Dhawan   (b) Vikram Sarabhai
   (c) A. P. J. Kalam   (d) U. R. Rao

372. Who wrote the prestigious award – winning book
Space Technology for Sustainable Development?
   (a) K.Kasturirangan   (b) Satish Dhawan
   (c) U. R. Rao   (d) R. R. Daniels

IX

CURIOSITIES

373. Who operated the first officially recognised rocket mail service?
    (a) Klaus Riedel   (b) Friedrich Schmiedle
    (c) Rudolf Nebel   (d) Fritz Stamer

374. Which eminent scientist claimed some years before the rocket was invented that it was not possible to build a rocket that could be launched into space?
    (a) Vannevar Bush   (b) Ernest Rutherford
    (c) Edwin P. Hubble   (d) Arthur S. Eddington

375. Who proposed the theory that Martian moons were spaceships launched by a long extinct civilization on that planet?
    (a) Carl Sagan   (b) I. Shklovskii
    (c) Fred Hoyle   (d) J. Allen Hynek

376. The name of this satellite was selected in a nation wide contest. Which was the satellite?
    (a) *Hipparcos*   (b) *Molniya*
    (c) *Anik*   (d) *Aryabhata*

377. Who first tried building a racing car driven by so lid-fuel rockets?
    (a) Fritz von Opel   (b) Arthur Rudolph
    (c) Max Valier   (d) F. A. Tsander

378. Which German space pioneer was consulted by a film company to build a rocket for their forthcoming film?
    (a) Max Valier   (b) Hermann Oberth
    (c) Rudolf Nebel   (d) Fritz von Opel

379. Which country's launches are restricted to some months in a year because they affect its tuna fishing industry?
    (a) India   (b) China
    (c) Japan   (d) USA

380. A giant cannon at Florida, USA, fires an aluminium bullet containing human passengers at the Moon. A century later, the *Apollo* spacecraft is launched from the same region. Which writer made this odd prophecy through his science fiction novel?
    (a) H. G. Wells   (b) Jules Verne
    (c) Kurt Lasswitz   (d) K. E. Tsiolkovsky

381. Who first tried building a glider powered by solid-fuel rockets?
   - (a) Gottlob Espenlaub
   - (b) Frank von Hoeff
   - (c) Max Valier
   - (d) Fritz von Opel

382. To gain the support of Americans in technology, a human voice was broadcast for the first time from a satellite in space in 1958. Whose voice it was?
   - (a) Wernher von Braun
   - (b) Albert Einstein
   - (c) James van Allen
   - (d) Dwight D. Eisenhower

X

POLITICS

383. Which US President had said quite some time ago, 'I believe that this nation should commit itself to achieving the goal, before this decade is out, of landing a man on the Moon and returning him safely to earth....'?
    - (a) John F. Kennedy
    - (b) Dwight D. Eisenhower
    - (c) Lyndon B. Johnson   (d) Richard Nixon

384. What does the Bogota Declaration of 1976 deal with?
    - (a) Near-earth orbit
    - (b) Geo-stationary synchronous orbit
    - (c) Molniya orbit   (d) Polar orbit

385. Who proposed the creation of a 'Common market in Space' in 1984 at The Hague?
    - (a) Margaret Thatcher   (b) Rajiv Gandhi
    - (c) M Mitterrand   (d) Mikhail Gorbachev

386. When did the United Nations create the Outer Space Committee to look after space affairs?
   (a) 1957   (b) 1960
   (c) 1958   (d) 1961

387. Which US President announced the country's National Space Policy?
   (a) John F. Kennedy
   (b) Dwight D. Eisenhower
   (c) Ronald Reagan   (d) George Bush

388. When did ministers of eleven member-countries of European Space Agency meet in Rome and agree to lend their hand in the development of the US Space Shuttle?
   (a) 1982   (b) 1983
   (c) 1984   (d) 1985

389. When did the United Nations Assembly give the 'Declaration of Legal Principles Governing Activities of States in Exploration and Use of Outer Space'?
   (a) 1966   (b) 1965
   (c) 1964   (d) 1963

390. Which US President gave the directive to build a permanent manned space station to maintain the pioneering spirit of the country?
   (a) Ronald Reagan   (b) Jimmy Carter
   (c) George Bush   (d) Richard Nixon

391. Which international body established a 'Committee On the Peaceful Uses of Outer Space' (COPUOS) in 1958?
    (a) UNESCO   (b) Friends of the Earth
    (c) UNO
    (d) World Resources Institute

392. Which country has set up a scheme called 'Sharing of Experience in Space' for training of scientists from developing countries?
    (a) China   (b) Japan
    (c) India   (d) USA

XI

ESTABLISHMENTS

393. Where is the US Eros Data Center which distributes *Landsat* and other remote-sensing data and pictures located?
    - (a) Nebraska
    - (b) South Dakota
    - (c) Florida
    - (d) California

394. Where is China's main space launch site, Shuangchengtzu Centre, located?
    - (a) Gobi desert
    - (b) Takla Makan desert
    - (c) Lu-ta
    - (d) Ning-po

395. Where are the tracking stations of the NASA's Deep Space Network located?
    - (a) Goldstone, Canberra, and Madrid
    - (b) Arecibo, Cheshire, and Nancy
    - (c) Tucson, Madrid, and Canberra
    - (d) Arecibo, Cheshire, and Brisbane

396. Where is Russia's mission control centre for space flights located?
   (a) Leningrad   (b) Baku
   (c) Sevastopol   (d) Kaliningrad

397. Where is the launch site of the Japanese Institute of Space and Aeronautical Science located?
   (a) Milisawa   (b) Tanagashima
   (c) Kagoshima   (d) Nanao

398. Where is the Gagarin Cosmonaut Training Centre located?
   (a) Near Leningrad   (b) Near Gorky
   (c) Near Moscow   (d) Near Kharkov

399. Where is the main launching site of the European Space Agency located?
   (a) Algeria   (b) Argentina
   (c) Ireland   (d) French Guiana

400. Where is the Space Telescope Science Institute, which will co-ordinate the research of and collect scientific data from the Hubble Space Telescope, located?
   (a) Oklahoma   (b) Denver
   (c) Kansas City   (d) Baltimore

401. Where is the European Space Agency's major research and test centre located?
    (a) France   (b) United Kingdom
    (c) Netherlands   (d) Belgium

402. Where is the Baikonur Cosmodrome, the main Russian launch site, located?
    (a) Near Astrakhan   (b) Near Sevastopol
    (c) Near Latvia   (d) Near Tyuratam

XII

INDIA IN SPACE

403. Where are the headquarters of the Indian Space
Research Organisation located?
    (a) Bangalore   (b) New Delhi
    (c) Ahmedabad   (d) Trivandrum

404. Which Indian space scientist has won the Marconi
International Fellowship for applying modern
communications technology to meet the needs of
isolated rural villagers?
    (a) Satish Dhawan   (b) Yash Pal
    (c) U. R. Rao
    (d) Vikram Sarabhai

405. What is India's rank in the race to enter space?
    (a) Seventh   (b) Eighth
    (c) Sixth   (d) Fourth

406. Where is the National Institute of Remote Sensing located?
    (a) Hyderabad   (b) Kolkata
    (c) Dehradun   (d) Chennai

407. When was the Indian Space Research Organisation set up?
    (a) 1949   (b) 1959
    (c) 1969   (d) 1979

408. Where was India's experimental communications satellite APPLE launched from into geo-stationary orbit?
    (a) Cape Canaveral   (b) Baikonur
    (c) Kourou   (d) Sriharikota

409. Where is the Indian Space Research Organisation's Master Control Facility for controlling the functioning of satellites located?
    (a) Sriharikota   (b) Nagpur
    (c) Car Nicobar   (d) Hassan

410. Where is the National Remote Sensing Agency that collects, analyses, and distributes data and pictures on various aspects of the country's landscape, located?
    (a) Hyderabad   (b) Kharagpur
    (c) Dehra Dun   (d) Jodhpur

411. When was the Thumba Equatorial Rocket Launching Station set up in the country?
    (a) 1957   (b) 1963
    (c) 1968   (d) 1972

412. Where is the satellite launching station of the Indian Space Research Organisation located?
    (a) Thumba   (b) Balasore
    (c) Hyderabad   (d) Sriharikota

413. When was the Department of Space to outline and plan space activities in the country established?
    (a) 1957   (b) 1963
    (c) 1972   (d) 1981

414. Where are satellites built in India?
    (a) Bangalore   (b) Trivandrum
    (c) Ahmedabad   (d) Hyderabad

415. Where is the Satellite Tracking and Ranging Station of the Indian Space Research Organisation located?
    (a) Sriharikota   (b) Balasore
    (c) Kavalur   (d) Hassan

416. When was the first sounding rocket launched from Thumba Equatorial Rocket Launching Station?
    (a) 1963   (b) 1973
    (c) 1983   (d) 1993

417. Which is the company set up to commercially market ISRO space products and services?
    (a) Space India Corporation
    (b) Antrix Corporation
    (c) Space Products Ltd.
    (d) None has yet been set up

418. Where are the ISRO's Liquid Propulsion Test Facilities located?
    (a) Shillong   (b) Aluva
    (c) Mahendragiri   (d) Nagpur

419. Where is the Vikram Sarabhai Space Centre located?
    (a) Ahmedabad   (b) Nagpur
    (c) Shillong   (d) Thiruvananthapuram

420. Where is the GRAMSAT pilot project in progress to provide developmental communications to about 800 villages in the country?
    (a) Orissa   (b) Karnataka
    (c) Meghalaya   (d) Chhatisgarh

421. Which day is celebrated as 'Satellite Technology Day' in India?
    (a) April 19   (b) February 28
    (c) January 1   (d) May 11

422. Where was the first earth station set up in the country?
- (a) Arvi
- (b) New Delhi
- (c) Dehra Dun
- (d) Hyderabad

423. Where is the Satish Dhawan Space Center located?
- (a) Balasore
- (b) Sriharikota
- (c) Mahendragiri
- (d) Thumba

424. When did the Indian-made GSLV-D1 launch GSAT-1 into a geo-synchronous orbit of the earth?
- (a) 1998
- (b) 1999
- (c) 2000
- (d) 2001

425. Which of the following satellites is not of Indian make?
- (a) *LANDSAT-1*
- (b) *OCEANSAT-1*
- (c) *CARTOSAT-1*
- (d) *METSAT-1*

426. Which is the series of sounding rockets developed by ISRO to conduct atmospheric research and other scientific investigations?
- (a) *Kalpana*
- (b) *Rohini*
- (c) *Bhaskara*
- (d) None as yet

427. When was the pioneering Indian National Committee for Space Research (INCOSPAR) set up?
- (a) 1967
- (b) 1980
- (c) 1954
- (d) 1972

428. Which foreign satellite was launched by an Indian
Polar Satellite launch vehicle in 1999?
(a) *KITSAT-3*   (b) *OCEANSAT*
(c) *DLR-TUBSAT*   (d) *ARIANE-2*

429. Where is the ISRO's Development and Educational
Communication Unit – acting as interface between
space and people – located?
(a) New Delhi   (b) Bangalore
(c) Ahmedabad   (d) Shillong

430. When did India place the *Rohini* satellite
successfully in an orbit of the earth?
(a) 1970   (b) 1980
(c) 1990   (d) 2000

431. Where is the Centre for Space Science and
Technology Education in Asia and the Pacific located
in India?
(a) Ahmedabad   (b) Dehra Dun
(c) Hyderabad   (d) Bangalore

432. Which ISRO centre offers Post-Graduate courses
in remote sensing, satellite communications, satellite
meteorology, etc.?
(a) SHAR Center   (b) VSSC
(c) CSSTE-AP   (d) SAC

433. When was the *GSAT-2* (Geo-synchronous Satellite-2) successfully launched by GSLV-D2 rocket launcher?
    (a) 2000   (b) 2001
    (c) 2002   (d) 2003

434. Which satellite's successful launched into space in 2000 is a milestone in India's space programme?
    (a) *INSAT-2C*   (b) *Bhaskara*
    (c) *INSAT-3B*   (d) *IRS-1*

435. What is the name of the Indian space mission to the Moon?
    (a) *Trishul-1*   (b) *Nag-3*
    (c) *Chandrayan-1*   (d) *Agni-4*

XIII

MISCELLANY

Futuristic

436. Which is the site in space favoured for future space colonies?
   (a) Larangian point-5
   (b) Lagrangian point-2
   (c) Larangian point-3
   (d) Lagrangian point-1

437. Which planet can be a source of fuel for any future interstellar spaceship?
   (a) Venus
   (b) Mars
   (c) Neptune
   (d) Pluto

438. Who could in future be used for sailing in the interplanetary space in a yacht-like spacecraft?
   (a) Solar radiation
   (b) Gravity
   (c) Vacuum
   (d) Temperature gradient

439. Which type of satellite will be mammoth in size?
   (a) Powersat   (b) Comsat
   (c) Radarsat   (d) Landsat

440. What will be used as a 'space tug' abroad a Space Shuttle in the coming years?
   (a) OTV   (b) OMV
   (c) OMS   (d) ORS

441. What is the futuristic HOTOL?
   (a) Spaceship   (b) Satellite
   (c) Orbiting station (d) Launcher

442. Which technology will be used in future space stations for collecting and distributing solar energy throughout them for illumination, recreation, and health?
   (a) Laser
   (b) Thermoelectric generator
   (c) Ceramics   (d) Fibre optics

443. What class of remote sensing satellites will India's Polar Satellite Launch Vehicle carry into space?
   (a) 350 kg   (b) 500 kg
   (c) 700 kg   (d) 1000 kg

444. Which year is designated as the 'International Space Year' by the International Council for Scientific Unions?
    (a) 1999   (b) 1995
    (c) 2002   (d) 1992

445. *Buran* is the name of a new spacecraft. What is it?
    (a) Space Shuttle   (b) Satellite
    (c) Spaceship   (d) Space probe

Other Than Space

446. Which of the following pairs of astronauts is husband-and-wife?
    (a) Robert Crippen and Anna Fisher
    (b) Robert Gibson and Rhea Seddon
    (c) Story Musgrave and Mary L. Cleave
    (d) Vance Brand and Sally Ride

447. Which rocket pioneer was deaf?
    (a) Robert H. Goddard   (b) K. E. Tsiolkovsky
    (c) Sergei P. Korolev   (d) Hermann Oberth

448. What was the cause of death of the first man in space, Yuri Gagarin, in 1968?
    (a) Aircraft accident   (b) Heart attack
    (c) Prolonged illness   (d) Spacecraft mishap

449. Which Russian space pioneer was executed in 1881 for possessing revolutionary literature?
   (a) N. I. Kibalchich   (b) Yuri Kondratyuk
   (c) I. T. Kleimenov   (d) Sergei P. Korolev

450. Which pioneer astronaut was burnt to death inside an *Apollo* spacecraft during training?
   (a) John Glenn   (b) Gordon Cooper
   (c) Neil Armstrong   (d) Edward White

451. Which space pioneer's book received a literary prize money that was subsequently invested in rocket research?
   (a) Max Valier   (b) Willy Ley
   (c) K. E. Tsiolkovsky   (d) Hermann Oberth

452. Which space pioneer was a university professor?
   (a) Robert H. Goddard   (b) Hermann Ganswindt
   (c) Krafte Ehricke   (d) Hermann Oberth

General

453. Which Russian satellite carrying a nuclear energy source crashed in Canada in 1978 causing worldwide concern?
   (a) *Cosmos-954*   (b) *Cosmos-1609*
   (c) *Cosmos-451*   (d) *Cosmos-1218*

454. Which optical telescope was launched into space in 1990?
   (a) Hooker telescope
   (b) Hale telescope
   (c) Hubble telescope
   (d) McMath telescope

455. Which bird was successfully tracked using a satellite?
   (a) Shearwater
   (b) Sea gull
   (c) Arctic tern
   (d) Albatross

456. Which one of the following satellite systems has drastically affected radio astronomical studies in recent times?
   (a) *GOES*
   (b) *INMARSAT*
   (c) *GLONASS*
   (d) *ISEE*

457. Which rocket launched the *Asiasat* in 1990?
   (a) Long March III
   (b) Ariane-3
   (c) H-I
   (d) Polar Satellite Launch Vehicle

458. Which main problem faced the Russian space station *Mir*?
   (a) Docking between spacecraft
   (b) Defective solar cells
   (c) Heavy load of equipment
   (d) In-orbit assembly

459. Which living being was born in space for the first time in 1990?
    (a) Honeybee   (b) Butterfly
    (c) Quail   (d) Monkey

460. What discipline of science the Indian technologist and President A. P. J. Kalam specialises in?
    (a) Nuclear technology
    (b) Aerospace technology
    (c) New materials technology
    (d) Automobile technology

461. Which astronaut performed his marriage ceremony through a phone while he lived aboard the International Space Station in assembly stage?
    (a) Marc Garneau   (b) Vladmir Remek
    (c) Yuri Malenchenko
    (d) Bruce McCandless

462. In which subject Kalpana Chawla specialised in before she became an astronaut?
    (a) Aerospace engineering
    (b) Civil engineering
    (c) Aeronautical engineering
    (d) All

463. How many European countries form the European Space Agency that co-ordinates their space projects?
    (a) 11   (b) 13
    (c) 8   (d) 9

464. Which developed nation has no involvement in space activities?
    (a) Australia   (b) Canada
    (c) Japan   (d) UK

465. Which country has three centres for launching rockets and spacecraft?
    (a) Japan   (b) India
    (c) China   (d) Italy

466. At what temperature is the liquid hydrogen maintained before it is fed to the main engines of a rocket to burn and drive it?
    (a) 0^0 C   (b) 20^0 C
    (c) 45 K   (d) 20 K

467. How many stable Lagrangian points are there in space?
    (a) Two   (b) Three
    (c) Four   (d) Five

468. Which American state has the Armstrong Air and
Space Museum containing objects associated with
Neil Armstrong's career?
  (a) Ohio   (b) Texas
  (c) Nebraska   (d) Indiana

469. Who piloted the *Apollo-11* command module which
orbited the Moon while the first man landed there?
  (a) James McDivitt   (b) Russell Schweickert
  (c) Michael Collins   (d) Eugene Cernan

470. Which is the most common rocket fuel?
  (a) Liquid oxygen
  (b) Ammonium perchlorate
  (c) Liquid hydrogen
  (d) Powdered aluminium

471. Where did the *Viking-I* spacecraft land on Mars?
  (a) *Utopia Planitia*
  (b) *Argyre Planitia*
  (c) *Chryse Planitia*
  (d) *Syrtis Major Planitia*

472. Which astronaut said, 'Art is important in comp-
rehending space because the photographs can't
duplicate the colours, the texture of being there'?
  (a) William Thornton (b) Vance Brand
  (c) Alan Bean   (d) William Lenoir

473. What is the velocity needed for a spacecraft to leave the Moon?
    (a) 7.1 km/ second   (b) 2.38 km/ second
    (c) 4.3 km/ second   (d) 11.2 km/ second

474. Which nation's first artificial satellite broadcast the music of 'The East Is Red'?
    (a) China   (b) Japan
    (c) India   (d) None

475. What drove the Lunar rover or buggy that *Apollo* astronauts used to survey the Moon surface?
    (a) Nuclear reactor   (b) Solar cells
    (c) Batteries   (d) All

476. At what temperature is the liquid oxygen maintained before it is fed to the main engines of a rocket for burning hydrogen and to drive it?
    (a) 90 K   (b) 70 K
    (c) 50 K   (d) 10 K

477. Where was the first International Astronautical Congress held?
    (a) London   (b) New York
    (c) Paris   (d) Moscow

478. Which body brought out *Who's Who in Aviation and Aerospace*?
    (a) Space Foundation
    (b) World Space Center
    (c) International Astronautical Federation
    (d) National Aeronautical Institute

479. How many astronauts landed on the Moon during the Apollo space programme?
    (a) Six   (b) Twelve
    (c) Eighteen   (d) Twenty

480. During the *Skylab* missions, two living beings, Anita and Arabella, were studied for their activities under zero-gravity conditions. Who were they?
    (a) Two monkeys   (b) Two mice
    (c) Two spiders   (d) Two ants

481. Where did the unmanned rover *Lunakhod-1* land on the surface of the Moon?
    (a) *Mare Crisium*   (b) *Mare Orientale*
    (c) *Mare Serenitatis* (d) *Mare Imbrium*

482. Who observed, 'Put three grains of sand inside a vast cathedral, and the cathedral will be more closely packed with sand than space is with stars'?
    (a) Jayant V. Narlikar (b) James Jeans
    (c) Heather Couper   (d) Nigel Henbest

483. What is the difference between a launch vehicle and a missile?
    (a) Payload   (b) Nose cone
    (c) Nozzles   (d) Countdown

484. What is the present annual growth rate of debris orbiting the earth?
    (a) 8.6 per cent   (b) 1.2 per cent
    (c) 12.6 per cent   (d) 5.6 per cent

485. What is the name of the International Space Station presently being assembled in space?
    (a) *Victory*   (b) *Freedom*
    (c) *Peace*   (d) *Joy*

486. Where are the preparations for living on the planet Mars in progress?
    (a) Mauritius   (b) Car Nicobar
    (c) Devon Island   (d) Devil's Island

487. Where is the International Space University located?
    (a) France   (b) Germany
    (c) Austria   (d) Russia

488. Where is the headquarters of the International Astronautical Federation located?
    (a) Munich   (b) Vienna
    (c) Paris   (d) Moscow

489. Who forwarded the concept of the Common Minimum Global Space Mission to tackle the crises of energy, water and minerals facing the mankind?
(a) Bruce Murray   (b) A.P.J. Kalam
(c) John Glenn   (d) George Bush

XIV

PHOTO QUIZ

490. Can you make out anything about this drawing? What is it? What is its purpose?

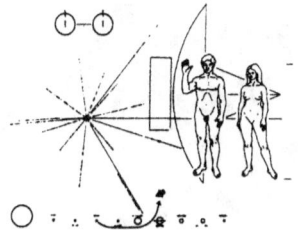

491. What is this antenna? What is it meant for? When was it used?

492. What is this structure? Which vehicle will assemble it? When is it likely to be completed?

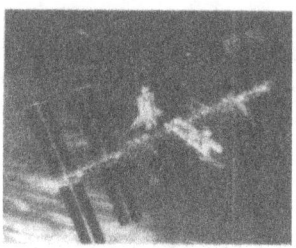

493. What is this funny action scene? Where is it being enacted? What is the purpose? Who are these persons?

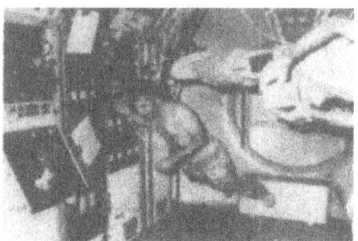

494. What is this strange vehicle? What is its purpose?

495. Is there anything special about this craft? What is it supposed to do? Which space body is building it?

496. Where is this rocket launching complex located?

497. Where is this small rocket being fired from?

498. Which is this Indian rocket?

499. Which is this space probe? Where is it landing?

500. What is this hat-like space probe?

ANSWERS

1. (a)
2. (a)
3. (d) A Czech.
4. (b)
5. (a)
6. (a) However, she died as Space Shuttle failed to launch into space.
7. (c) A French.
8. (a) and (b) Both monkeys.
9. (a) A journalist.
10. (c)
11. (a)
12. (d)
13. (a) Co-pilot of the first Space Shuttle flight.
14. (a)
15. (a)
16. (a) First to set his foot on the Moon.
17. (d)
18. (a)
19. (c)
20. (b)
21. (c)
22. (b)
23. (b)
24. (b) European Space Agency's first astronaut to fly abroad the Space Shuttle.
25. (d)
26. (c) Renamed 'Mechta' (Dream)
27. (d)
28. (b) *International Cometry Explorer*
29. (c)
30. (b)
31. (d)
32. (c)
33. (d) Indian Satellite.
34. (a) and (d) are names of the same spacecraft launched from Japan.
35. (d)
36. (b)
37. (a)
38. (d)
39. (c)
40. (d)
41. (d)
42. (a)
43. (b)
44. (d)
45. (b)
46. (c)
47. (b)
48. (c)
49. (b)
50. (a) Pen-name of Hermann Potocnik, an Austrian army officer.
51. (c) and (d)
52. (a) and (b)
53. (a)
54. (c) and (d) Observed effects of rotating centrifuge on mice.
55. (b)
56. (d)
57. (c) Originally German.
58. (a)
59. (a)
60. (d)
61. (b)
62. (b)
63. (b)
64. The European Space

Agency's Ariane-3.

65. The Russian Proton.

66. The Japanese H-2 Nippon.

67. The Chinese CZ-3.

68. (b)

69. (a)

70. (a)

71. (c)

72. (c)

73. (b)

74. (a)

75. (c) On Baltic Sea, Germany.

76. (a)

77. (c) Used for Apollo programme.

78. (b)

79. (b) and (c)

80. (a) and (c)

81. (c) Weather satellite is placed both in geo-stationary as well as polar orbit.

82. (d)

83. (d)

84. (a)

85. (c)

86. (c)

87. (c)

88. (d)

89. (a) and (d)

90. (a)

91. (c)

92. (a)

93. (c)

94. (b)

95. (d)

96. (c)

97. (a)

98. (b)

99. (a) A Space Shuttle

100. (c)

101. (c) and (d)

102. (d)

103. (a)

104. (c)

105. (d)

106. (b)

107. (b)

108. (d)

109. (b)

110. (a)

111. (c)

112. (c)

113. (c) Formation of a charged layer around it as the shuttle enters atmosphere.

114. (b)

115. (d)

116. (c)

117. (b)

118. (a)

119. (c) In the lower terrestrial atmosphere.

120. (c)

121. (d)

122. (b)

123. (c)

124. (c)

125. (b)

126. (d) Like a glider, it has to make a perfect landing the first time.

127. (a) and (c)

128. (a)

129. (c) and (d)

130. (a)

131. (b)

132. (b)

133. (c)

134. (b)

135. (c)

136. (b)

137. (b)

138. (a)

139. (a)

140. (d)

141. (b) Gagarin went into space aboard this spacecraft.

142.(d) Called 'Gemini capsule', the astronauts were collected from the sea.

143.(d)

144.(a) Launched into space by a Space Shuttle.

145.(c)

146.(c)

147.(b) With its Payload Bay doors open.

148.(c) Stretched Rohini Satellite series.

149.(d)

150.(a)

151.(b) and (d) Named in honour of Arthur C. Clarke who conceived of it.

152.(a) The earth being the parabola's focus.

153.(b)

154.(d)

155.(d) 40,000 km by 500 km.

156.(a)

157.(d)

158.(b)

159.(c)

160.(d)

161.(a)

162.(d)

163.(d)

164.(d)

165.(a) or (b) Liquid Cooling Garment is the modern term for Constant Wear Garment.

166.(b)

167.(a) Call sign of the Mission Control at Houston, U.S.A.

168.(b) Sometimes, Polaris is also used.]

169.(c)

170.(a)

171.(d)

172.(c)

173.(d)

174.(c)

175.(a) In the early days of spaceflight, baby food was eaten.

176.(c)

177.(a)

178.(a) and (b)

179.(b)

180.(c)

181.(d) See quiz no.182..

182.(c)

183.(d)

184.(b) and (c)

185.(c)

186.(b) An aircraft provides that for about half a minute during a parabolic trajectory.

187.(a)

188.(c)

189.(c)

190.(a) and (b)

191. All factors are taken into account.

192.(b)

193.(a)

194.(b)

195.(c)

196.(a)

197.(c) and (d)

198.(c)

199.(b)

200.(b)

201.(c)

202.(b)

203.(d)

204.(c)

205.(c)

206.(a) A prototype not meant to fly into space.

207.(c)

208.(c) *Minimum Orbital Unmanned Satellite of Earth.*

209.(b)

210.(b) High Energy Astronomical Observatory

211.(a) Adopted from a science fiction.

212.(c) Space Transportation System.

213.(a)

214.(a)

215.(c) Called 'Long March' after the 1927 historic march .

216.(a)

217.(d)

218.(d)

219.(c) EMU.

220.(a)

221.(a)

222.(b) EVA.

223.(b)

224.(a)

225.(a) and (d) In addition to other routine house-keeping jobs in the shuttle.

226.(a)

227.(a) and (b)

228.(a) and (b)

229.(c) and (d)

230.(d)

231.(a)

232.(d)

233.(c)

234.(d)

235.(b)

236.(b)

237.(c)

238.(c)

239.(d) Main launch site of NASA, where space shuttles are launched.

240.(b)

241.(c)

242.(b)

243.(c) This effect is observed during the firing.

244.(d) Anti-Satellite.

245.(d)

246.(a) It is the transporter of the shuttle.

247.(c)

248.(b)

249.(c)

250.(c)

251.(d)

252.(d)

253.(b)

254.(c)

255.(a) Rockets came to the notice of the Britishers, who developed them further for warfare.

256.(c)

257.(c)

258.(a)

259.(a)

260.(a)

261.(d)

262.(a)

263.(a)

264.(b)

265.(a)

266.(d)

267.(b)

268.(d) Yuri Gagarin entered space on that day.

269.(b)

270.(b)

271.(a)

272.(d)

273.(b)

274.(b) Acronym in German.

275.(a)

276.(d) Founded in Moscow but was

short-lived.

277.(c)

278.(a)

279.(c) Office of Space and Terrestrial Applications.

280.(d) National Space Development Agency.

281.(b)

282.(b)

283.(c) At the fifth Lagrangian point.

284.(a) Houston, USA

285.(b) Houston, USA

286.(c)

287.(b)

288.(d)

289.(b)

290.(c)

291.(a)

292.(a)

293.(a)

294.(a)

295.(a)

296.(d)

297.(d)

298.(b)

299.(c)

300.(b)

301.(a) Project was abandoned due to nuclear test ban treaty.

302.(a)

303.(d)

304.(b)

305.(d)

306.(a)

307.(b)

308.(b)

309.(b)

310.(b)

311.(d)

312.(d)

313.(a) In 'Don Juan'.

314.(b)

315.(c)

316.(c)

317.(d)

318.(d) Adolf Hitler feared the world would come to know about rocket developments in Germany through the film.

319.(c)

320.(c) 'Voyage a Venus'.

321.(d) 'The Brick Moon'.

322.(c)

323.(a)

324.(a)

325.(b)

326.(a)

327.(a) and (b)

328.(b)

329.(b)

330.(c)

331.(a)

332.(d)

333.(b)

334.(c)

335.(d)

336.(d)

337.(c)

338.(a)

339.(b)

340.(a)

341.(c)

342.(b)

343.(a)

344.(c)

345.(b)

346.(b)

347.(b)

348.(c)

349.(c)

350.(c)

351.(b)

352.(d)

353.(c)

354.(d)

355.(b)

356.(b)

357.(b)

358.(a)

359.(c)
360.(b)
361.(a)
362.(b)
363.(a)
364.(a) Describes her frustration in not entering space finally.
365.(d)
366.(d) Deals with space colonies.
367.(c)
368.(c)
369.(c) Published as 'The Goddard Biblio Log'.
370.(a)
371.(c)
372.(c)
373.(b) Service operated in an Austrian mountainous region.
374.(a)
375.(b)
376.(c) Means 'Brother' in Eskimo language.
377.(c)
378.(b) Willy Ley, the writer, was also consulted.

379.(c)
380.(b)
381.(c)
382.(d)
383.(a)
384.(b) The equatorial countries claimed that this orbit should be considered a part of their territory - and not outer space.
385.(c)
386.(c)
387.(c)
388.(d)
389.(d)
390.(a)
391.(c)
392.(c)
393.(b)
394.(a)
395.(a)
396.(d) Baltic coast.
397.(c)
398.(c) Called 'Star city'.
399.(d)
400.(d) Maryland.
401.(c) Called 'European Space and Technology Center' at Noordwijk.
402.(d) Southern

Russia, west of Aral Sea.
403.(a)
404.(b)
405.(a)
406.(c)
407.(c)
408.(c)
409.(d) In Karnataka.
410.(a)
411.(b)
412.(d) Island in the Bay of Bengal.
413.(c)
414.(a)
415.(c)
416.(a)
417.(b)
418.(c)
419.(d)
420.(a)
421.(a) The launch date of India's first satellite 'Aryabhata'.
422.(a)
423.(b)
424.(d)
425.(a)
426.(b)
427.(c)
428.(a) and (c)

429.(c)

430.(b)

431.(b) At the Indian Institute of Remote Sensing.

432.(c) See Quiz no.431.

433.(d)

434.(c)

435.(c)

436.(a)

437.(c) Its atmosphere contains hydrogen.

438.(a)

439.(a) Huge solar arrays, several square kilometers in size.

440.(b) Orbital Manoeurving Vehicle.

441.(d) Horizontal Take-Off and Landing rocket.

442.(d)

443.(d)

444.(d) 500th anniversary of Christopher Columbus's voyage to the New World.

445.(a) Russian Space Shuttle.

446.(b)

447.(b)

448.(a)

449.(a)

450.(d) He was the first American to walk in space.

451.(d) The Road to Space Travel.

452.(a) and (d)

453.(a)

454.(c)

455.(d)

456.(c)Transmits several radio frequencies.

457.(a)

458.(d)

459.(c) Aboard the 'Mir' station.

460.(b)

461.(c)

462.(a)

463.(b)

464.(a)

465.(c)

466.(d) Or – 253 degree C.

467.(a)

468.(a) In the hometown of Armstrong.

469.(c)

470.(c)

471.(c)

472.(c)

473.(b)

474.(a)

475.(c)

476.(a) Or – 183 degree C.

477.(c)

478.(d)

479.(b)

480.(c)

481.(d)

482.(b)

483.(a)

484.(a) Average for three years.

485.(b)

486.(c)

487.(a)

488.(c)

489.(b) many things from this drawing about human beings and the earth.

490. Message for any alien being engraved on the plaque of the US *Pioneer-10* spacecraft which has already left the solar system. An alien intelligence should be able to make out many things from this drawing about human beings and the earth.

491. A part of the Satellite Instructional Television Experiment (SITE) conducted in India in 1975.The antenna is of the Transportable Remote Area Communications Terminal meant to catch TV signals coming from a satellite and re-transmit them to neighbouring areas.

492. An artist's view of the International Space Station being assembled in space at present.

493. Interior of the ESA's 'Spacelab' launched by the Space Shuttle into space. The crew is conducting zero-gravity experiments of benefit to the humanity in shirtless environment.

494. 'Lunar Rover' on the Moon. It could move at the speed of 13 km per hour. Used by 'Apollo' missions to survey some regions and collect Moon rocks.

495. The European Space Agency's Space Shuttle-like space plane called 'Hermes'.

496. The ISRO's Shar Launch Complex at Sriharikota, now renamed 'Satish Dhawan Space Centre".

497. The Indian sounding rocket RH-300 in flight, launched from Thumba.

498. Polar Satellite Launch Vehicle of the ISRO.

499. *Galileo* space probe near Jupiter.

500. The Mars Polar Lander undergoing tests in a laboratory.

SCORE YOURSELF!

Count the correct answers you have given and mark yourself as follows:

Average: if 400-424 answers are correct.

Good: if 425-449 answers are correct.

Excellent: if 450-474 answers are correct.

If you score more than 475, you are a **SUPER GENIUS** in space.